One Weekend in Seattle

Marie Tuhart

www.marietuhart.com

ONE WEEKEND IN SEATTLE

by. So please, if you find a typo or any formatting issues, please let us know at marie@marietuhart.com so that we may correct it.

Thank you!

Acknowledgements

Laurie, for critiquing and helping me make the book better.

Red Quill Editing team, you are the best team to work with.

Lissane Jones for the invitation to contribute to the One Weekend world.

Publisher's Note: No Artificial Intelligence was used in the writing of this book.

Blurbs

Strangers to Lovers
One Weekend
Passion Reigns

Newly divorced Gabby Maxwell is ready to celebrate her newfound freedom, and hitting the clubs with her friend is the perfect solution. Her night out takes an unexpected turn when a mysterious and alluring stranger asks for a dance. The pain of her divorce makes her mistrust men. Despite her caution, Sawyer evokes a desire she hasn't felt in years. Her body wants him, but her mind isn't so sure it's a good idea to spend time with him.

Against his better judgment, jaded billionaire Sawyer York is completely captivated with Gabby and her down-to-earth nature. The chemistry between them grows stronger as he indulges her love of food and her job as a chef. He shows her the best Seattle has to offer. The day leads into a romantic evening and an explosive night of intimacy.

He's begun to care deeply for Gabby, and the more time he spends with her, his guilt eats at him. He's with held vital information.

When secrets are uncovered, Gabby realizes she was right not to trust Sawyer.

Sawyer knows he has his work cutout for him to show Gabby he's willing to give up everything to have her in his life.

Chapter One

The car share dropped Gabby and Lindsay off next to a modest brick building. With her preoccupation over how quickly her life had changed, Gabby had no clue where they were in Seattle, but she trusted her best friend to know how she wanted to celebrate tonight. The line of glitzed up ladies and gentlemen extended around the corner. The place must be very popular.

"Come on." Lindsay grabbed her hand, and they walked past the line of people to the front of the building.

Gabby Maxwell looked up at the small sign above the door. *The Vault*. "How did you find this place?"

Lindsay always found new places to go out for the night. Up until now, Gabby's life had been stilted, and she'd lived vicariously through her best friend. Their weekly phone calls were full of Lindsay's stories. Truth be told, Gabby had been a little jealous of Lindsay's freedom.

"I know the bartender. Come on." Lindsay led her to the entrance where a bouncer stood. "Hi, Lindsay Collins and guest."

The bouncer looked at his phone. "Yes, Ms. Collins. I have you here. I need to see IDs for you and your guest, please."

Gabby opened her purse and pulled out her driver's license. Luckily, she'd placed it where it was easily accessible. The bouncer took it from her, looked at it, and back at her. He also held it up to the light and ran his fingers over it before handing it back to her. He did the same with Lindsay's.

"Perfect. Please go in and give your name to the host; she will seat you." He unclipped the velvet rope, and they walked through.

"I'm impressed." They'd just passed probably a hundred people in line on a Friday night.

The host smiled when they walked up to the desk. Her name tag read *Maggie*. The dance music was going, and Gabby glanced up to where she could see the DJ on the second floor.

"Welcome to The Vault."

"Hi. Lindsay Collins."

"Welcome, Ms. Collins." Maggie looked at a list. "If you'll follow me." She slipped from behind the counter and walked off.

Lindsay giggled, and they followed. Gabby looked around as they walked. The place was bigger than it appeared from the outside. There was a huge dance floor, a long bar, areas roped off, tables and chairs in another area, plus stand-up tables in another.

She looked up to where the DJ stood on the second floor and noticed plush chairs, sofas, and small tables, all separated by glass panels. Interesting. The hostess unhooked a velvet rope and walked up two stairs to the raised area and gestured to the right. It was a half booth with high back black leather seats.

Lindsay slid around the table as Gabby sat and shifted toward the middle. "There are menus and a drink list on the table. Your server will be with you shortly."

"Holy crap." Gabby couldn't help her exclamation. This place was totally unexpected.

"I'll have to thank Jesse."

"Jesse?"

"My bartender friend."

Gabby glanced toward the bar. There was one man behind it. He was a big enough guy that he could be a bouncer. He wore black pants and a white shirt with no sleeves. When he glanced up, he nodded and grinned. Gabby wasn't sure what that meant. Also, he didn't look like Lindsay's type. "Is that him?"

Lindsay looked over at the bar. "No. He's probably in the back. Let's see what they have for food." She grabbed the menu and laid it on the table between them. "I'm starving," Lindsay said.

"Me too. You picked me up from the airport, went to your apartment, where you gave me just enough time to change, and now we're here." So the man who grinned at her from behind the bar wasn't Jesse. That made Gabby feel a little better. Her friend had a habit of picking the wrong men. Gabby sighed. Who was she to talk?

"Well, don't blame me. Your flight didn't arrive until seven."

"It was the first flight I could get at last minute." Expensive as well. Not that she cared. The fight was over, and she wanted to celebrate her freedom with her best friend.

"Let's get a bottle of Moet to celebrate," Lindsay commented.

Gabby glanced at the menu. Her eyes widened. "It's three hundred dollars a bottle." She shouldn't have been surprised at the price; they were in a high-end nightclub.

"No worrying about cost tonight. I'll take care of it."

"Lindsay..." she started to protest.

"No." Lindsay held up her hand. "It's a small price to pay now that you're finally divorced from that loser. Besides I've been saving for this day."

Gabby couldn't argue. It had taken so long to get the divorce because her ex wouldn't respond to anything. "I have money to help pay." It wasn't like she'd spent anything in the last two years except essentials and a divorce lawyer. Not that divorce lawyers were cheap, but Gabby had a job that paid really well.

"No, I've got it. How about the beef sliders, fries, and charcuterie board."

Gabby's stomach rumbled. "All sounds good."

"Evening, ladies." A muscled young man in black pants and a white sleeveless shirt commented. "I'm Brad. What can I start for you tonight?"

"Hi, Brad." Lindsay had a wide grin on her face. Gabby shook her head. Her friend flirted with everyone. Not that Brad wasn't good looking. He just wasn't Gabby's type.

Lindsay gave their order and asked for water. Brad nodded and left. More people began filling the place. "I still don't get how we got this amazing booth."

"Jesse arranged it. This is one of the VIP booths. When you called and told me the divorce was final, I called Jesse. We were lucky. There was a cancellation, and Jesse put us down. This place is constantly at capacity."

Gabby swallowed. "The line outside?"

"General admission, they open at ten for them. The VIPs have some private time."

"Interesting." It was. Gabby had never been to a place like this. "I'll have to thank Jesse."

"No big deal. He told me it's one of the perks of his job."

Gabby nodded, but wondered if that was true. Not that she attended a lot of nightclubs. Her job as an executive chef didn't allow a lot of down-time. Fourteen-hour working days didn't give her too much leisure time.

"Gabby, don't worry about anything this weekend. I want you to relax and enjoy. You've done nothing for the last three years but focus on your job. This is your weekend to let go and rejuvenate."

"You're right." She'd been separated for almost two years and trying to get a divorce for a year. In all that time, she'd done nothing but concentrate on her job. It was time for a change. But tonight wasn't the time to talk about it. Tonight was about celebrating her freedom.

Brad returned at that moment. He opened the champagne and poured it into two crystal flutes. "I'll be back with your food soon."

Lindsay picked up her glass. "To freedom."

"To freedom." They clinked the stemware and took a sip. Light bubbles teased her taste buds. White peach and apple notes unfurled, and the sweet citrus flavors lingered. "This is delicious."

"I knew you'd like it."

Gabby nodded as she began to relax. This was what she needed: a night out with her best friend. Tonight was for fun.

***

Sawyer York looked down at the crowd. "Looks good tonight," Eric, his friend and business partner, said.

"It always does on the weekend." It was ten o'clock, and the club was bustling as the general admission patrons entered. He enjoyed watching the people talking and looking around in awe. The excitement he'd felt when he first opened the club had somehow become tarnished. He'd opened The Vault five years ago after he sold off the technology company he'd created.

The sale made him an instant billionaire. And all the vultures came out of the woodwork. Sawyer shook his head. He was becoming so cynical at thirty-five. Maybe it was time for a new venture.

"Before I forget, Jesse asked if he could take one of the VIP booths tonight, and I said yes. We didn't have a reservation for it."

"We didn't?" That was odd; the VIP booths were usually snapped up.

"The party canceled, and I didn't see any harm since Jesse said it was for his friend and her friend to celebrate some big event in their lives."

"Which one?" Sawyer was curious.

"Number one."

Sawyer's gaze moved to the booth. From where he stood on the second floor, he could see the two women in the VIP section. One of the women was laughing, her head thrown back, her black hair with red highlights cascading past her bare shoulders. One of the lights flashed on her face. There was a carefree light in her features. He forgot how to breathe as she picked up her champagne flute and clinked her glass to the other woman's and drank.

For a second, Sawyer glanced at the other woman, but his gaze immediately went back to the dark-haired woman companion. His cock tightened. *Whoa.* When was the last time he'd had a reaction to a woman like that? Years.

"The blonde is Jesse's friend," Eric said.

Sawyer spared him a glance, and his friend laughed.

"It's written all over your face. You're interested."

"Doesn't mean I'm going to do anything."

"Why not? Come on, Sawyer, you've been living like a monk."

"You know why."

"Gina was a first-class gold digger and bitch."

Sawyer couldn't argue with that. "And I let myself be blinded by her." He wasn't proud that she'd somehow strung him along perfectly. He'd always thought he was smarter than that.

"Gina was good, but in the end, she showed her true colors."

"True." Sawyer's gaze returned to the woman in the booth. What was it about her that held his attention? Brad, one of the servers, went up to the table with several plates and arranged them on the table.

The woman Sawyer was intrigued by gestured to the food and chatted with Brad. It seemed like she was asking about the food. Sawyer wished he could hear the conversation. Brad walked away, and she picked up one of the sliders and took a bite. Her eyes closed as she chewed.

Sawyer couldn't help himself; he was entranced by this woman. He kept his gaze on her face as she swallowed, and pleasure lit up her expression. His gut tightened. He was restless tonight. Something was missing from his life. When had he become so disenchanted?

When he opened the nightclub, he'd decided to offer food along with drinks. Some thought he was crazy to offer more than snacks, but he found people enjoyed having food with their drinks. Not that they had an extensive menu, mainly finger food and salads. They made the *real* money on the alcohol.

Sawyer glanced out at the crowd again. Maybe he'd take a walk on the main floor.

He glanced over at the DJ. He'd decided to keep the DJ on the second floor. It kept people from coming up to the DJ with requests, but it was also where he and Eric shared a big office in the opposite corner.

The rest of the second floor was turned into seating for any of his or Eric's special guests who didn't want to be on the main floor. They could enjoy the view and talk in private or go downstairs and dance if they wanted. Investors who knew Sawyer and Eric often wanted a place they could take clients to that was more causal than a formal restaurant. Sawyer didn't mind. They paid him well for it.

"I'm going to go walk around downstairs," he said.

"Enjoy." Eric grinned at him, and Sawyer ignored him. It wasn't unusual for one of them to walk the floor and check in on things.

***

Gabby took another drink of her champagne, sated and relaxed. The sliders were perfect, the fries crisp, and charcuterie board was great, a mixture of cheeses, fruit, crackers, and jam. It was everything a person could want in a nightclub. Simple, but with flavors that pleased the senses. At least for her.

The dance floor was semi-crowded, but the place was hopping. "How did you meet Jesse and find out about this place?"

"I met Jesse a few weeks ago on one of the singles outing groups I went with. We started chatting, and he told me where he worked. When the weekend rolled around, I stood in line and came into the club."

"That line was enormous."

"Jesse told me it's always like that. People want to be seen at The Vault."

"Why is that?" Gabby was curious.

"Probably something to do with the billionaire owners." Lindsay waved her hand toward the DJ area. "Not that I cared about that. Jesse is so much fun."

"Ah." Gabby wiggled her eyebrows at her friend.

"Stop." Lindsay slapped Gabby on the arm and laughed.

"Evening, ladies."

The silky-smooth whisky voice drew Gabby's gaze. Her breath caught in her throat. *Holy crap!* Seattle knew how to find sexy men. He was well over six feet in her estimation. His dark hair was cut short. And those intense blue eyes... It was like looking into ocean waves.

"Hello," Lindsay said.

"Good evening," he said before he held his hand out. "Would you like to dance?"

"Me?" Gabby's mouth dropped open. Men always went for her blonde bombshell friend. Not that it bothered her. She was always happy Lindsay had the attention.

"Yes. Shall we?"

Lindsay elbowed her in the side, leaned over and whispered, "Go have fun."

Gabby swallowed and placed her hand in his. Heat flared as he helped her to her feet. With her hand in his, he kept her tucked close to him as they navigated to a spot on the dance floor. He turned her into his arms with care as the music turned slow.

His arms snaked around her waist, and she placed her hands on his wide shoulders. He kept his hold soft, yet she felt safe and cared for. A wave of heat filled her body. She'd never felt this drawn to someone before. She followed his lead, and when the song changed, she remembered where she was.

"I'm Gabby, by the way."

He smiled, stealing the breath from her lungs. "Hi, Gabby. I'm Sawyer."

Lord, she loved the timbre of his voice when he said her name. The music was now lively, and they danced with the others on the floor. It was a little hard to talk, but at least she got his name. Sawyer. Nice. It fit him. The next song was slower, and he took her into his arms and began to sway.

Her skin tingled as he held her. This was unusual. She'd dated a few times during her separation, and no one had made her feel like Sawyer did at this moment.

"I hope it's okay I stole you away from your friend," he said.

"You did ask."

"I did. My mother raised me to be a gentleman."

Her mind swirled with her instant attraction to this man, so much so, she realized she was biting her lip. She had no clue how to respond.

They danced from one song to the next, sometimes making small talk and other times not.

"I need to sit down," Gabby said after the eighth song. She wasn't used to being in heels, even if they were only one inch.

"Of course." He led her from the floor back to her table, but it was empty. Gabby glanced at the bar and saw Lindsay wave at her.

"Since my friend is talking with her boyfriend, would you like to join me?" It seemed the right thing to do. Besides, she'd like to know more about this man.

He looked at the bar and then back at her. "I'd like that."

Gabby slid into the booth, and Sawyer followed. His thigh touched hers, and a shiver of awareness flowed through her body.

"What can I get for you, sir?" Brad asked when he approached their table.

"Walker Blue Label, neat. And can you refresh the charcuterie board, please."

"Of course, sir." Brad picked up the board. "Ma'am?"

"I'm fine." There was still a half bottle of champagne and water on the table.

Brad nodded and left.

"You didn't need to do that," she told Sawyer.

"I get the munchies when I drink." He flashed her a grin. "Tell me, Gabby, what brought you to The Vault tonight?"

"My friend. I flew in today, and she brought me here to celebrate."

"Celebrating a birthday? New job?"

"Neither." Gabby usually wasn't this honest with someone she just met, but Sawyer struck her as a straightforward man. "My divorce was finalized on Wednesday."

His eyes widened.

"I'm not on the rebound," she added quickly. Gabby didn't want him to think she was out looking for a new man. "To make a long story short, we've been separated for three years. I've been trying to divorce him for a year, and the court finally stepped in and granted my divorce when he wouldn't respond to anything."

"Sounds like a great guy." The sarcasm in his voice was evident.

"We drifted apart." Gabby was somewhat sad her marriage ended the way it had, but when she looked back on it, her ex was the one who encouraged her to become an executive chef then complained about the hours.

"What about you? What brought you to the club tonight?"

He hesitated before answering. "I'm one of the managers here."

Why did he pause? Was he worried she would look down on him for being a manager? "Shouldn't you be working?" Gabby ducked her head and covered her mouth with her hand. "Sorry, that was rude."

He laughed. A deep, rich laugh that sent quivers over her skin. "It's fine. I'm not the only one on duty tonight. The other manager can handle things."

Brad arrived with his drink and the fresh charcuterie board. He set them on the table before leaving.

"Do you mingle with the patrons a lot?" Gabby picked up a piece of cheese and popped it in her mouth, enjoying the sharp cheddar flavor.

"Not usually." He took a sip of his drink. "I normally watch to make sure there are no issues and handle any problems at the bar or in the kitchen."

"I bet you're overworked and underpaid."

He didn't answer. "What type of work do you do?"

"I'm an executive chef."

"I'm not sure our food lives up to your standards."

The dryness of his words made her laugh. "Trust me, it's good. I may provide fancy food where I work, but I prefer down-to-earth things, and your sliders especially were very good."

"That's nice to know."

"Have you lived in Seattle long?" she asked. She wanted to know more about Sawyer. There was this invisible string between them, and it tightened each time he spoke. Maybe Lindsay was right; she needed to let herself go for once.

***

Sawyer sat back against the leather cushions of the booth. Gabby had no idea who he was. While that surprised him, it also delighted him. It was so rare for him to have anonymity. He was glad for it. She was a refreshing breeze, and it also reinforced his decision to get to know her better.

"I've lived in Seattle most of my life. You said you flew in today, where from?"

"San Francisco Bay Area." She took a drink of water. "I don't live in San Francisco—too expensive—but outside the city."

He nodded. Seattle wasn't cheap by any means. "Your friend lives here?"

"Yes. In West Seattle."

"And when do you go back to the Bay Area?" How much time could he spend with her this weekend? Oh yeah, he was thinking of spending time with her. From their short discussion so far, he saw she was more genuine than most of the people he knew, let alone the women. And damned if he didn't want her back in his arms. He hadn't wanted to leave the dance floor.

"Monday." She sighed.

"You don't want to go back?" Was it because of her ex? Or something else?

"Yes and no." She shook her head. "You probably don't want to hear this."

"I do." He was fascinated by her.

"I'm burned out at my job is all. I'll figure it out." She waved her hand. "What do you do when you're not working at the club? If I remember right, it's only open Thursday through Sunday."

"You're right; it's only open four days, but there are still things to do during the week. Ordering food, beverages, making sure we have personnel. Paying vendors and other bills. It's never-ending."

"I get that. Being at the restaurant at six in the morning to take in food deliveries, and staying until after the dinner rush. It gets old."

Sawyer groaned. "Those are long days." They continued to chat about their shared food issues, laughed and talked about deliveries and all the things that went wrong. He realized they had a lot in common.

"Is this your first trip to Seattle?"

"In a way. I visited Lindsay when she first moved up here, but it was more to help her find a place and figure out what she needed. Sometimes that girl is helpless with the day-to-day stuff."

Excitement filled him as an idea formed in his mind. "You've never played tourist?"

"No."

"If you're free, would you allow me to escort you around Seattle tomorrow? Show you what it has to offer?" Maybe she'd consider moving here. Wait a second. What was he thinking? They just met. But something deep inside said he should get to know her better, and he wanted that more than he'd wanted anything in quite a while.

Gabby tilted her head, and all he could think about was lowering his lips and tasting her sweet skin. "I'd like that, but I need to check with Lindsay."

"Check with me for what?" Lindsay said, causing Gabby to jump.

Lindsay stood with her arms braced on the silver railing. She was smiling. "Hi, I'm Lindsay." She extended her hand out to him, her expression curious.

"Sawyer." He shook her hand. "I was asking Gabby to let me take her around Seattle tomorrow." Lindsay's hazel eyes lit up, as she and Sawyer turned expectant gazes to Gabby.

Gabby shrugged. "I didn't know what you had planned."

"Nothing." Lindsay turned to Sawyer with a smile after a mischievous glance at Gabby. "I'm going to say she'd be delighted to see Seattle with you."

"Lindsay." Lindsay laughed at the outrage in Gabby's voice.

"I'll be at the bar." Lindsay sashayed away, waving her fingers in the air.

Sawyer breathed a sigh of relief. Lindsay didn't seem to recognize him.

"I don't think I was ever that carefree," Gabby commented.

"That's a shame," he whispered. "Tomorrow?" He didn't want to press her, but he really wanted to spend time with her.

"Lindsay has given her seal of approval, so yes, I'd love to see Seattle with you."

"Wonderful." He took her hand, raised it to his lips, and kissed her knuckles. "We're going to have a marvelous time."

"You sound very sure of that."

Sawyer laughed. "I am." Gabby not knowing who he was made him more relaxed and would allow him to show her Seattle without any expectations.

The music slowed, and he took Gabby's hand. "Let's dance."

She slid out of the booth with him, and on the dance floor, he pulled her into his arms, grinning like a fool. The DJ always played some slow songs during the night, and Sawyer planned to take advantage of each one. Gabby flowed into his arms as they moved around the floor.

Each touch of her body against his made his dick pulse. His body was reacting in ways he didn't expect. "Is there any place in particular you'd like to go tomorrow?"

"Pike Place Market, if you're not sick of taking people there." Her voice was soft.

He gazed down at her. "You got it." He liked Pike Place. "There are so many unique vendors and food."

She smiled. "I'm always up for good food."

"Part of the executive chef job?"

"In a way."

There was a wishful tone in her voice. "Care to tell me?"

Gabby lowered her gaze. "It's not important."

"Ah, but I think it is." He swung her around, creating a little separation from other couples on the floor.

"Really, it's no big deal."

Sawyer frowned. It didn't sound right to him. He opened his mouth to dig deeper, but backed off. They really didn't know each other that well...yet. For now, he'd be content with holding her in his arms and dancing.

***

Gabby took a deep breath as she slid back into the booth. What was it about Sawyer that made her want to bare her soul? She hadn't dated much during her separation. Was that the cause? She'd only had, what, two glasses of champagne, and she'd also eaten and made sure to drink water. She wasn't drunk, so her reaction to him didn't make sense.

Dancing those slow dances, being chest to chest and hip to hip with Sawyer, made her wonder if she'd gone too long without sex. It was an odd thought, but damned if she didn't want to explore with Sawyer. But she was only here for the weekend. Unless she moved up here like Lindsay wanted.

She slammed on the mental brakes. No. It was too early to think about that with Sawyer. On the drive to the club, Lindsay had encouraged her to keep an open mind and relax a bit. Gabby was trying. After years of working her ass off, relaxation was hard for her.

Her phone pinged. "Excuse me." She pulled it out of her purse. A text message from her boss asking about the Saturday delivery. With a sigh, she texted him back and glanced at the time. It was almost midnight.

"Everything okay?"

"Yes. Just a quick work question. For tomorrow, where and when should I meet you?"

"I'll pick you up."

"There's no need to drive to West Seattle just to drive back this direction."

Sawyer stared at her. "Remember earlier, when I mentioned my mother raised me to be a gentleman? I can pick you up. A little extra drive is not going to kill me."

Just that quick, Gabby's insides melted. When was the last time anyone offered to pick her up? Certainly not her ex, who never cared how she got home from work on late nights. "Okay." She wasn't going to argue with him, and she disliked city driving anyhow. It was nice not to worry about getting around.

"Good. Tell me Lindsay's address please. I'm assuming you're staying with her."

"I am, but I need to check with her first."

"I understand. Can I get your phone number?"

"That I can do." She waited until he pulled his own phone out before rattling off her number. A second later, her phone pinged.

"That was me, so you'll have my number."

Gabby looked up as Lindsay wobbled over. "How are you two doing?" While Lindsay's words were clear, Gabby had a feeling her friend had had a little too much to drink.

"Good." It was time to get Lindsay home. "What time tomorrow do you want to pick me up?"

"Is eight-thirty too early?"

"I can do that."

"Oh good, I'm glad you two are spending time together," Lindsay commented with a big grin.

"Yes. And I think it's time to go home."

Lindsay pouted but didn't protest.

"I'll walk you out to your car," Sawyer said as they walked toward the entrance.

"We came by ride share," Gabby said.

"Let me call one for you." He pulled his cell out and stepped away.

"I like him," Lindsay said.

"Me too." She glanced at her friend. "How much did you have to drink after the champagne?"

"Oh just a few shots at the bar with Jesse. Sooooo, Sawyer is picking you up tomorrow."

"Yes. Is it okay to give him your address?"

"Always so concerned about safety," Lindsay said. "Yes, it's fine."

"Car will be here in a few minutes," Sawyer said, walking up to them.

Lindsay swayed, and Gabby gripped her arm. "I think she's had too much to drink."

Sawyer smiled. "It's okay." He took her other arm, and they moved outside.

The lines were gone, but the bouncer was still at the door. The cool Seattle evening brushed over Gabby's arms. Maybe she should have brought a cover-up.

"Here."

Warmth enveloped her as Sawyer draped a jacket over her shoulders. Her heart melted. Such a gentlemanly thing to do.

"Seattle can get a little chilly at night. Remember that for tomorrow."

"Thank you. I've texted you Lindsay's address."

"Perfect." He smiled, and Gabby's knees wobbled.

Thankfully, a car pulled up right in front of the building at that moment. "I didn't think anyone was allowed to drive down this road?"

"Before midnight, no, but after, it's all good." Sawyer opened the back door.

"Wait a second, this isn't a ride share," Gabby said.

"It's a service I work with all the time." Sawyer helped Lindsay into the vehicle and turned to her. "I promise they're very reputable."

"But..." He placed his fingers on her lips.

"Please don't worry so much. I promise you and Lindsay will be fine. I wouldn't risk any woman's life."

Gabby sighed. "I'll try." She shrugged off the jacket and handed it to him. "Thanks for the jacket loan."

"You're welcome. And Gabby?"

She turned her head.

"Until tomorrow." He brushed a soft kiss over her cheek before helping her into the car and shut the door.

The front passenger window rolled down, and Sawyer gave the driver Lindsay's address and stepped back. The car moved, and Gabby turned to watch out the back window until the vehicle turned, and Sawyer disappeared.

"Are you ladies comfortable?" the driver asked.

How could they not be? The smooth black leather seats molded to their bodies, and there was enough room for eight people. "We're good, thank you," Gabby replied.

He nodded.

"So tell me about Sawyer." Lindsay's words were slightly slurred, but the look on her face was intensely curious.

"What is there to tell?"

"You're going to spend the day with him?"

"Yes. He's going to show me Seattle."

"Did he say where he's taking you?"

"We talked about Pike Place Market." Gabby frowned. "Oh damn, I didn't bring a lot of clothing."

"Easy fix. If you need something, we're close enough to the same size you'll be able to borrow something of mine."

"Maybe." Gabby pulled out her phone and sent Sawyer a text about what she should wear. He texted her back less than a minute later.

Casual. Where we will be having dinner doesn't have a dress code, so don't be worried. Don't forget a jacket.

She chuckled as her thumbs tapped the screen. *"Yes, sir."*

"What's so funny?" Lindsay asked.

"Sawyer reminded me to bring a jacket tomorrow."

Lindsay nodded. "You like him."

"He's different." He was, and Gabby liked that. He wasn't at all pretentious like the people who came into the restaurant where she worked. It was a plus that he was so sexy. She shook her head, not sure if she was ready to jump back in the water yet. No sense getting ahead of herself. They'd just met.

Lindsay grinned. "I've seen him somewhere before."

"Where?"

"I don't know. It'll come to me." Lindsay laid her head against the seat and closed her eyes.

Gabby watched the lights of the city, thinking about tomorrow. She was looking forward to seeing Seattle with Sawyer, and she made a promise to herself that she would enjoy herself. No worries about her life, work, or anything else. This time was for her.

Chapter Two

♥

Sawyer stepped out of the car on Saturday morning and looked at Gabby's friend's apartment building. This was a nicer area of West Seattle. He stared at the security gate. Gabby hadn't given him the apartment number, so he pulled his cell out.

"Hi, Gabby. I'm downstairs."

"Hi! I'll be right down."

The line went dead, and he frowned. The gentleman in him bristled at not picking her up at her door. He paced until Gabby walked out to the gate.

"Sorry, I forgot about the gate, and Lindsay is still sleeping."

That explained why she didn't want him in the apartment. Her concern for her friend was admirable. His gaze took in the black pants combined with a red blouse. Her green eyes sparkled. There was a light jacket thrown over her arm. "No worries. May I say you look delicious." He leaned in to kiss her cheek.

Her cheeks bloomed. "Thank you. Is this going to be okay?" She indicated her outfit, which gave him a reason to appreciate curves in all the right places.

"Perfect." He took her by the elbow, guided her over to the car, and opened the door.

Gabby slid in and said good morning to the driver. "Same as last night."

"I told you I use the service a lot." His thigh touched hers after he shut the door. "Plus, parking in Seattle is no fun." He glanced at the driver. "Pike Place Market, please."

"Yes, sir."

"Did you sleep well?" he asked as the vehicle pulled away from the apartment building.

"Better than I expected."

"Oh. Hard to sleep when it's not your own bed?"

"That was part of it." She glanced at him and then away. "I was excited about today."

"I'm glad." He hid a smile. "I want you to be excited, and I hope you enjoy everything I have planned."

"What do you have planned?" She faced him once again, her face alight with anticipation.

"First is Pike Place Market, and we'll spend several hours there."

"And after that?" Gabby squirmed in her seat.

"You'll have to wait to find out."

She frowned at him, before her face lit up. "Is that the baseball and football fields."

Sawyer glanced out the window. "Yes, it is." They were making good time. Thankfully, it was early enough on a Saturday there wasn't a lot of traffic.

The driver avoided the tunnel and took the surface streets. Gabby continued to look out the window. They passed the building he lived in, but he didn't point it out.

"Your club is down that street, right?"

"Yes."

"You're so close to Pike Place. You must go there a lot."

"Believe it or not, I don't."

"Too touristy?"

"Sometimes, but for you, I'm willing to risk it." He'd risk a lot more than that for her. That thought floored him. Somehow, in the last twelve or so hours, Gabby had captured a part of him that made him want to do things he wouldn't do with others.

"You're so sweet."

The driver chuckled, and Sawyer's eyebrows rose as he caught the driver's gaze in the rearview mirror. "Ma'am, he's anything but sweet." The man grinned in the mirror. "Sorry, sir."

Sawyer shook his head. "He isn't wrong."

"Doesn't matter." Gabby waved away Sawyer's remark. "I think you're sweet."

The driver turned onto Pike Place Road and found an empty spot. "I'll pick you up at Virgina and Western at two."

"Perfect. Thank you." Sawyer climbed out and helped Gabby out. He glanced at his watch. "We need to hurry." He took her hand, and they walked across the street.

He stopped outside of a café and smiled at the person waiting there. "Are you the York party?" the man asked.

"Yes, that's us."

"Great." The young man smiled. "Go inside and order a coffee, if you'd like; they'll start handing out samples and give their talk." He held the door open, and they walked inside.

"Café and chocolate?" Gabby gazed up at him with a wide smile.

It wasn't like she couldn't smell the coffee and chocolate. "Yes. Our first duty of the day is a food tour."

Her eyes widened. "A food tour?"

"Yes. What else would I do for a foodie?"

Gabby smiled, and threw her arms around his neck. "This is perfect."

He was surprised by her exuberance and pleased by her openness. "Let's order. I could use more coffee."

Sawyer got a black coffee and Gabby a vanilla latte. They gathered around a table with the others in the tour as a worker came out with a tray. "Good morning, everyone. I have some samples of our chocolates."

Gabby glanced around. There were only six other people. This was a small tour group compared to what she'd done before. She plucked a piece off the tray, and Sawyer grabbed one. She took a nibble. "This is so creamy and one of the best chocolates I've ever tasted."

"Only the best for you."

***

Gabby listened to their guide, Ian, who talked about how they produced their own chocolates and had classes for everyone who wanted to learn as she nibbled on chocolate and drank her coffee.

A food tour? She hadn't expected that. She figured they'd walk around the marketplace, maybe see a few shops and leave. After encouraging them to buy items when they returned after the end of the tour, Ian guided them to their next stop.

"How did you arrange this so quickly?"

"I know people."

"I hope it wasn't too expensive to do last minute." Gabby wasn't sure she liked the idea of Sawyer calling in favors or owing favors for her.

"It wasn't. And please stop worrying. This is nothing."

She opened her mouth to argue, but Sawyer touched her lips with his finger. Tingles shot through her.

"No more arguing; otherwise, I'll be forced to kiss you in front of all these people."

"I dare you." Gabby stopped walking. "I can't believe I said that."

He chuckled. "You don't have to dare me at all. I want to kiss you." He nudged her forward so they could catch up with the group. His hand rested on her low back—the intimacy of the contact not lost on her. Even such a simple touch excited her.

"I want that too."

"Later." His gaze blazed. "For now, just enjoy."

She took a deep breath. He'd gone to so much trouble to do this for her, and she was going to enjoy every second of it.

Two hours later, they were back where they started. Sawyer guided her to a table and held a chair out for her, before he went to get them something to drink. When he returned, he had coffee for himself. "I brought an orange spice tea for you since you commented earlier it sounded interesting."

"Thank you." She blew on the tea and took a sip. The flavor soaked into her taste buds, a little sweet, but not overly so. "The tour was so good. Seeing the vendors throw fish around, all the fresh produce. The cheddar biscuits were to die for, and the smoked salmon... All of it was delicious."

"I'm glad you approve. Once we've rested a bit, we'll walk around the rest of the market. I have a list of shops I think you'd like."

"When did you do all this?"

"Early this morning."

"I'm not sure how you managed."

"Trust me. It's nothing."

"I don't think it's nothing." She reached across the table and placed her hand on the back of his. "This is all very thoughtful, and I appreciate it."

Sawyer turned his hand over and closed his fingers around hers. "I'm having fun. Drink up so we can continue our journey."

Their next stop was a nut vendor. "Oh my goodness! So many." Gabby loved nuts and incorporating them into food.

"Which ones would you like to sample?" Sawyer asked after he talked with the worker.

"How many can I sample?"

"As many as you want."

Her eyes widened with surprise. "Okay, I want to try caramel cashews, toffee peanuts, bourbon pecans, and maple sugar walnuts."

"I'll get a taste of the ghost pepper peanuts and coconut almonds."

"Of course, give me just a minute."

"You're living dangerously."

"I am?"

"Ghost pepper peanuts." She shuddered.

Sawyer leaned down, his eyes twinkling with mischief. "Spice is always fun. I have a feeling you can be very spicy."

The softness of his words sent a shiver over her spine. "You have no idea." Gabby bit her lower lip. She wasn't used to flirting like this, but she was enjoying herself.

After trying the samples, Gabby had a hard time deciding what she wanted. Besides the ones she tried, she wanted some other flavors.

"Get whatever you want."

"It's hard. They all taste good."

"Which ones are you thinking about."

Gabby listed six that she wanted.

"I'll tell you what, think about it, and we'll stop back before we leave."

"That might help. I might be able to narrow it down." She glanced across the way. "I'm going to go look at the produce too." Gabby turned away, hoping she could narrow down her choices. It wasn't like she couldn't afford to get them all, but she really didn't need that many nuts.

With a shrug, she began looking at the produce. Maybe find some fruit or something special to take to Lindsay.

***

Sawyer waited until Gabby moved on to the produce across the way before he ordered a half-pound of each of the ones she wanted, plus some for him. Gabby would probably object to him buying her nuts, but he didn't care.

His life was about business, and most of his relationships were—for lack of a better word—transactional. For the first time in his life, he was happy to spend money. There was no quid pro quo. She brought out the protective side of him he'd almost forgotten about.

"Ready?" he asked, coming up next to her.

"Yes." She glanced at his empty hands. "You didn't buy anything?"

"I bought what I wanted and told them I'd pick it up later. I'm not as indecisive as you are."

"I'm not indecisive; there are just so many."

Sawyer shook his head. "I think you'll enjoy the next place." He took her hand. Sawyer enjoyed holding her hand, another first for him. He'd never been much into public displays of affection, but with Gabby, it was different.

Their next stop was closed. "I'm sorry. I didn't realize they were closed on Saturdays."

"No worries. Their cooking classes look very interesting. I'll have to remember that. What's next?"

"Right around the corner." They made their way to the next stop, and her eyes lit up once again.

"This is great," she commented as they entered the kitchen store. "I'm going to go look around."

Sawyer released her hand. The store wasn't that big. There were multitude of shelves with all sorts of items on them. Gabby was like a kid in a candy shop. He could only smile at her happiness.

Forty-minutes later, they were on to their next stop. The pasta shop. Gabby's reaction didn't disappoint.

"I love pasta." She started going around to see what she could find. Sawyer followed her and made note of everything she picked up. These were all great ideas for future gifts. He froze at the thought of a future with Gabby. It wasn't like him to have thoughts like this, but Gabby made him feel... He couldn't find the right word.

She did pick out two oil sauces. "Why those two?" he asked.

"They are the two I want to try the most." She picked up the sample bottle. "Smell this one."

"I'm getting garlic."

"Yes, roasted garlic avocado oil. It would go good with pasta. Now this one." She held up a second sample bottle.

He wrinkled his nose.

Gabby laughed. "Mission fig balsamic, a little strong but would go great on a salad."

He nodded. When he went to pull out his credit card for her purchases, she stopped him. "No, Sawyer." She handed her credit card to the clerk. "I can pay for myself."

"But..."

"No buts." She stared at him. "I will pay for what I want."

He nodded but knew later today she was going to have a big surprise. He'd already texted his driver to pick up his bag and hers from the nut place. Of course, the purchase was before he knew she was so insistent about paying for her own stuff. Sawyer fought against having her pick out more for him to buy. He wanted to spoil her with every fiber in his body.

Patience, he reminded himself. "Our next stop is across the street. Why don't you head on over. I forgot to buy something."

"All right." She put her credit card away and took her bag from the clerk before leaving the shop.

"Can I help you, sir?"

"Yes. Do you have gift certificates I can buy online?"

"Of course." The clerk handed him a card. "You can also order anything from the store."

"Great." Sawyer took the card and left.

Across the street, he found Gabby chatting with one of the employees in the next shop.

"There you are," she said, motioning him over. "Try this wine and tell me what you think." Gabby handed him the wine glass.

Sawyer took a sip. "Nice Syrah."

The worker's mouth dropped open, and Gabby stared at him. "How did you know that?"

"Remember, I run a nightclub; I know wine. This has a berry flavor, along with savory notes. Syrah also tends to be darker than normal red wine. Quite good."

"Thank you, sir. We buy it from a winery in Eastern Washington."

"Lots of good wines here in Washington." Sawyer put the glass on the table. "We showcase several Washington wines at the club."

He turned to Gabby. "Have you looked around yet?"

"No. So many things." Her bright eyes lit up as she glanced around the store, ending with her gaze squarely on him. "Thank you, Sawyer. You know how to make my day special." Gabby moved away. There was no way he was going to get away with buying her anything in this store.

"Do you have gift certificates?" This made it possible for him to shower her with gifts at a later time.

"Yes, sir."

"Good. Also, do you do wholesale?" They really did have a lot of good wines.

"I believe so, sir. It would be best to talk with the owner. If you'll give me a moment, I'll get her."

"Thank you."

"Sawyer, they have truffle powder and salt, and...oh my, black truffle honey. I'm in heaven."

He grinned. Sawyer turned as a woman walked out from the back. He talked to her about doing a wholesale order for the club. The owner was excited, and he told her he'd follow up on Monday and took her business card.

Sawyer joined Gabby. She was like a kid in a candy store, and it made him happy. She ran her fingers over the bottles as she wandered around, picking one up here and there. At times, there was a wistful look on her face when she put the bottle back.

When was the last time he'd enjoyed Pike Place? A long time. It was usually crowded, and Sawyer wasn't one for crowded places, especially where he could be recognized. But today was a good day; no one seemed to care who he was, and Gabby was having the time of her life.

"We've got two more stops before we need to be at our pick-up spot in an hour."

"Okay." She grabbed a business card before they made their way out of the shop. "What's our next stop?"

"Across the next street." He guided her to their next stop.

"This is interesting." She gazed at all the spreads, honey, and chocolate sauces. "I want one of everything, but that's not possible."

"I can make that happen." The words slipped from his mouth.

Her eyes widened, and she tilted her head, staring up at him. He waited for her to explode or to ask him how he could afford to buy her everything in the store. One slip of the tongue could cause waves and explanations he wasn't ready for.

"That's a kind offer." Gabby laid her hand on his arm. Warmth spread through him. "You're giving me so much with this tour." She picked up the store's business card and looked at the person manning the stand. "You do ship, correct?"

"Yes, ma'am. Is there anything you want to sample?"

"No, thank you. It all looks so wonderful." She smiled at the clerk. "Where to next?"

Sawyer breathed a sigh of relief he hadn't messed up. "It's a little bit of a walk from here." He wanted to get her a gift certificate now as a surprise, but their next stop was several blocks away, and he didn't want her walking by herself. He grabbed a business card. More gift certificates for Gabby or maybe he'd just buy stuff and have it shipped to her.

"Okay." She slid her hand down his arm and entwined her fingers with his.

Sawyer enjoyed holding her hand. Together, they walked past the other vendors. He led her to a doorway and angled to the right. She squealed when she saw the shop name.

Gabby squeezed his hand. "You are the best."

"Go." He released her hand and watched her practically dance into the cutlery shop. She made her way to the row of display cases and began talking with the clean-cut young man behind the counter. Sawyer stood nearby.

He barely understood what they were talking about. He knew it was about knives, but all the lingo went over his head. While they spoke, he pulled out his cell, purchased a gift certificate from the last store, and purchased one from the one they were in.

His phone pinged with a text from his driver, letting him know he was on his way to pick them up. Sawyer made his way back into the store. Gabby was talking a mile a minute as the shop worker placed a knife inside a box.

"What did you get?" Sawyer asked.

"A Sabatier chef knife. I've wanted one of these for years, but they're expensive. Luckily, it's on sale today. I can't wait to add this to my collection." She handed her credit card over to the clerk.

"How will you get it home? You can't take it on the plane, and I don't think it would be safe in your checked luggage."

"Luckily, they ship." She grinned. "This has been the best." Gabby went up on her toes and brushed a kiss over his cheek.

His skin tingled from the contact. A simple kiss, but his body reacted, and damned if he didn't want to buy her the store. She was so happy with little things. Once the transaction was completed along with confirmation when it would be shipped, they left the store.

"Don't forget we need to go get our nuts."

Sawyer grinned. "Already done. I had my driver pick up the order for both of us."

"I told you..."

He put his fingers on her lips. "Please, it's a little thing for me to do for you."

She looked like she was going to protest as he took his hand away, but she shook her head and said, "Okay."

He blew out a breath, and they continued walking. Just as promised, his driver was waiting at Virgina and Western. Sawyer handed the bags he took from Gabby to the driver who put them in the trunk.

Gabby slid into the car with a sigh. "I admit I'm glad to sit down for a bit."

"It's good we're going to have lunch before our next walk." The vehicle pulled away from the curb.

"I admit I'm hungry."

"Well, it is two in the afternoon, and the food tour ended several hours ago."

"Where are we eating?"

"An Irish pub near our next adventure."

***

Gabby looked over the menu and couldn't decide what she wanted. Funny how she'd never eaten in an Irish pub before. She dreamed of visiting Ireland one day.

"Good afternoon. Would you like something to drink?" the server asked.

"I'll have an iced tea."

Sawyer ordered a beer on tap.

"I don't know what to order," she said, looking at Sawyer. Lord, this man took her breath away every time she looked at him. His hair was a little mussed, and he was totally relaxed—as he'd been all day.

He'd taken what little information she'd given him last night and crafted a day around a career she loved. She couldn't remember a time when anyone had done that for her.

"Dinner won't be until later tonight, so pick something that will keep you satisfied."

The word *satisfied* hung in the air. The waiter returned with their drinks. "Are you ready to order?"

"Do you have any suggestions?" she asked.

"You can't go wrong with shepherd's pie, beef stew, or fish and chips. Everything here is good."

"I don't know."

"How about this," Sawyer said. "Get the shepherd's pie, and I'll get the beef stew, and we can share."

"Deal." She put her menu down.

"Did you want the pint size, sir, or imperial?"

He glanced at Gabby. "Make them pint. I have a feeling that's going to be more than enough."

"Very good, sir. The food will be out shortly." The server picked up the menus and left.

"Pint or imperial?"

"Yes, basically small or large."

"Got it. I wonder if Lindsay knows about this place. She'd love it." She glanced around at the dark wood. The place was on the small size, but cozy and fun looking. "What are we doing after lunch?"

Sawyer reached across the table and took her hand in his. Something he'd been doing a lot today, not that she hadn't taken his hand a time or two. Her ex wasn't one to hold hands, and in a way, she'd gotten used to not being touched, but with Sawyer, it was different. Heck, with him, everything was different.

"I'm not going to spoil the surprise."

She laughed and shook her head. "You and your surprises."

"I promise you'll love what I have planned."

"How can you be sure of that?" She was intrigued by his confidence.

"How am I doing so far?"

Gabby closed her eyes and took a breath. "Batting a thousand, but I think you know that."

"I hoped that's what you'd think."

"Why hasn't some woman snatched you up by now?" Her voice held disbelief. The second she asked the question, she knew she'd made a mistake. A shiver skated over her skin as his facial features froze, and a frown appeared on his forehead. "Forget I asked."

Instantly, his features cleared. "It's okay." He squeezed her fingers. "I haven't found a woman who fits me. Yet."

"I have to say I'm surprised."

"Why is that?"

"You don't need me to spell it out." Gabby cursed herself for going down this path. Part of her wanted to know more about his man, but also, her attraction to him was growing by the second, and now she'd have to tell him exactly why.

He cocked his head. "Please do. I want to know."

She nibbled at her lower lip for a moment. "You're a handsome man."

"Looks aren't everything."

"True. But...You're so normal. Down to earth. Nice."

"What does that mean?" His voice held a note of disbelief.

"It means, you have a job in a nightclub that you seem to enjoy but you don't brag about. You don't mind showing someone around Seattle even though you've probably done it a thousand times." She took a sip of her tea. "You care about people. You put a lot of thought into what we are doing today based on what little I told you about myself last night."

"I care about you."

Gabby gulped, her insides swirling. "I-I care about you too."

They stared into each other's eyes for a long moment. When his eyes dipped to her lips, Gabby wanted him to kiss her more than she'd wanted anything in a long time. Except they were just getting to know each other. She didn't want to ruin this by jumping in feet first. Against her heart's wishes, she sat back in her chair.

Sawyer's eyes darkened for a moment, but a quick nod was the only other reaction he showed. He took a sip of his beer. "What else?"

What else could she say about him? That she wanted his lips on her. All over her. That she'd hardly slept last night thinking about their date? "Well, you understood when I told you not to spend your money on me."

Sawyer leaned forward. "First off, I rarely play tourist in Seattle. Second, it was obvious last night you like food, and I took that as a challenge."

"Right. The men I've known would override all my objections and do what they wanted anyway, but you haven't. You listen. That's a woman's dream man."

"Is it yours?"

Gabby glanced down at the table. Her cheeks heating. "At times."

"Will you tell me what your dream man is like?"

She shook her head. He squeezed her fingers until she looked up at him.

"Please. I'd like to know."

"A good listener would be one quality."

***

Guilt rose in Sawyer. He hated that he hadn't told her the truth, but he hadn't lied either, only kept the information private.

"A man who knows how to share his life." Her voice was soft.

"Share how?" This was interesting.

"I know men don't like to share their feelings, but sometimes their partner needs to know if something is wrong."

Sawyer cursed her ex-husband. Whatever their marriage had been like, the man had really done a number on her. Was there more to it than just the ex? "I agree with you."

Her eyes widened. "I also expect honesty."

Another hit to his conscience. "I do too." He did, especially after he got rid of Gina, who lied to him constantly. That had gutted him, and now he was guilty of lying by omission. How could he justify what he'd left out about his life?

He shook the guilt away. Gabby would understand. He hoped. Women flocked to him because of his money and his looks, but none wanted to know him. More than anything, he wanted a woman who cared more for him as a partner than for his money. He was so tired of gold-diggers. Gabby was a refreshing change.

"See. A woman's dream man." She shifted in her seat. "What do you want in a woman?"

Sawyer was surprised by the question. "No one has ever asked me that before."

"Will you tell me?"

He couldn't exactly say. "Some of the qualities you mentioned. I would also expect fidelity."

"That's a given."

Did he dare bare his soul to her? Something told him he was safe to do so. "I want a woman who sees me."

She tilted her head. "I'm not sure what you mean."

Well, he put his foot into it with that statement. He could just tell her, but it would probably ruin their day. It would wait. "Some, not all, women come to the club, see me, and figure I'm rolling in money." Not that he wasn't, but that would come out later.

"Shallow women."

He laughed. "You're so refreshing."

"I'm serious. There's more to a man than his pocketbook."

He didn't know how to respond and was grateful when the waiter showed up with their food. The smell of beef tickled his nose. "Ah, lunch."

The food was placed on the table, and the waiter left. Gabby looked down at her food. "This is a small?"

"Irish have a different idea of small and large."

"Thank goodness you didn't order the large." She picked up the big soup spoon that came with her meal and dug in. "Oh, my, goodness. This is delicious." She took another bite.

Sawyer ignored his own food to watch Gabby. On her second bite, she closed her eyes. "This is so delicious. The spices combined with the gravy mix well. I never would have expected lamb and parsnips to taste this good together."

"Why not?" He was curious.

"Maybe because it's ground lamb and not beef, but it works." She glanced at his meal. "Aren't you going to eat."

"Yes." He dived into his food and enjoyed the beer infused beef. They ate in silence for a few minutes until he lifted a healthy portion on his fork "Taste."

"One second." She took several sips of water. "I needed to clean my palate." Gabby reached for the utensil he was holding.

"Oh no. Open."

Eyes wide, she leaned forward and allowed him to feed her. Her lips closed over the food, and she closed her eyes. "Oh my. The beer is so flavorful, and the gravy works so well with mashed potatoes."

"I'm glad you like it."

"Your turn." She held out a spoonful of her food.

Sawyer had no issues with her feeding him. He opened his mouth, but when she slid the spoon into his mouth, he captured her wrist. He slowly pulled the spoon from his mouth all the while caressing her wrist. Her cheeks went pink as she pulled her hand back.

"Delicious," he said after he swallowed.

"I need to learn to make these dishes."

"I'm sure you'll excel at it."

"You're going to give me a swelled head."

"Not possible." He grinned, and they went back to eating. Maybe, one day, he'd taste Gabby's cooking.

After lunch, Sawyer took her hand again, and they walked a couple of blocks and into a building with a sign proclaiming "Underground Tour."

"Underground?"

"Yes, you haven't experienced Seattle until you've done the underground tour."

***

Gabby blinked as they exited the tour. "That was fascinating." She smiled at Sawyer. "I never knew about the original downtown."

"Many people don't."

"And walking over the skylights, and seeing them from underground. So interesting, but so scary."

"What was scary about it?"

"All those people probably don't know what's beneath them."

He nodded.

"Where are we going now?" she asked as they walked down an alleyway. It was funny. She never would have done this by herself, but with Sawyer at her side she felt safe.

"A special place." They crossed the street, down another alleyway, and turned. After barely a few steps, Sawyer stopped.

"Welcome to the waterfall garden."

Gabby stepped past the entrance and blinked. "A waterfall?" A beautiful waterfall cascaded down over the rocks. The sound was soothing...and hypnotic.

"Let's sit for a few minutes, and you can enjoy this lush domain."

Sawyer led her to a stone bench. She sat, her eyes never leaving the waterfall. There was something so soothing about water cascading down, not only watching it but hearing it. Gabby had no idea of how to explain it.

They sat there in silence for a bit until Sawyer shifted. "We need to go."

Gabby sighed. "Thank you." She brushed a kiss over his cheek before he helped her to her feet. "This was so relaxing."

"Good. Now for our next stop of the day." He guided her out of the park to where the car waited.

"When did you call him?"

"I didn't." Sawyer opened the door and allowed her to slide into the vehicle.

"But..."

He slid in, and Gabby forgot her words as his thigh touched hers. It had been like that all day. A single touch, holding hands, thighs brushing. Her body short circuited each time.

"I gave him our timeline."

"Sneaky man."

"You have no idea."

Gabby gazed out the window. The scenery was mostly businesses, but she did see some apartments and the Seattle Public Library building. They made several turns and stopped at a light.

Wait a second. "The Space Needle," she said softly as it came into view.

Sawyer grinned. "In all its glory."

The car went straight ahead and into the loop. No parking signs graced the area. "Out we go." Sawyer opened the door and helped her out. He leaned in the open door and told the driver he'd text him when they were done.

The door was shut, and Gabby turned and looked up. "Why couldn't I see this before we got here?"

"Too many buildings in the way." He guided her along the walkway. At the entrance, he pulled out his phone and showed the tickets, and they walked in. "We have about an hour and a half before our dinner reservation."

"Where are we eating dinner?"

"You'll see." They moved into a room that displayed the history of the Space Needle. Gabby was fascinated by how they built the Needle and the history of it. All too soon, Sawyer guided her toward the elevator.

"Can we take a picture?" she asked upon seeing a photographer. It would be nice to have a picture to remind her of this day.

"Sure." They posed for the picture and then made their way into the elevator.

Gabby clung to Sawyer's hand as the elevator ascended.

"You okay?" he whispered.

"Yeah. Just a little nerve-racking going up this high in a glass elevator."

"I promise the view will be worth it."

The elevator came to a smooth stop, and Gabby took a breath. They exited, turned right, and climbed a set of stairs to the upper observation level. Sawyer put his arm around her waist and guided her outside.

The view was amazing. Floor to ceiling glass. "This is...breathtaking." She moved up to the glass and glanced out. Sawyer moved up beside her and slipped his arm back around her waist.

He pointed out several Seattle landmarks to her. They walked around and got a great view of the city. All too soon, he guided her back down to the enclosed observation desk and to the elevator. Sawyer led her over to another elevator.

"Another elevator?"

"Yes." He gave his name, and they were allowed into the elevator and whisked up. When the doors opened, she lost her breath.

"This is the rotating restaurant." Gabby almost couldn't believe it. "You are the best." Without thinking, she threw her arms around his neck and gave him a quick kiss on the lips.

"Evening, ma'am, sir," the host said.

Gabby jumped like someone had burned her. Where was her decorum? Out the window apparently. Sawyer was making her dreams come true.

"Reservation under York."

"Of course. This way." The waiter guided them into the restaurant.

Gabby looked down and gasped.

"Gabby?"

"The floor is glass." It was hard to breathe.

"Yes."

"Is it safe?" she whispered.

"Very." He drew her to his side. "I would never do anything that put you at risk."

Her heart slowed, but her knees wobbled as they made their way to their table. Of course it was a glass table. She settled on the round chair. They had a fantastic view.

"Your waiter will be here with your first course shortly."

"Are you afraid of heights?"

"Not really." She smiled at him. "As long as I look straight out, I'm fine. The floor threw me."

"They remodeled several years ago and added the glass floor, but I can assure you it's safe."

"When did you get your engineering degree?"

"I minored in engineering, but I know the group that built this."

Ha! He'd called her bluff. Gabby relaxed in the chair. "That does make me feel a little better."

"Concentrate on the view straight out, or better yet…" He shifted his seat so he was seated next to her rather than across from her. "Concentrate on me."

He slid his arm over the back of her chair, and her nerves came to life. How could she concentrate on anything with him sitting so close to her?

Gabby cleared her throat. "The host said the first course."

"Yes." He rubbed her upper arm. "It's pretty much a pre-fixed menu. I ordered what I though you would enjoy."

"You haven't been wrong so far." It was uncanny how this man found things that made her happy and excited. It was like he could read into her deepest wishes, but that wasn't possible.

"Good evening." Their waiter set water goblets on the table. "I'm Tony, and I'll be your server tonight. In a few moments, I'll bring out your first course of Yukon gold potato chips with shaved black truffle and vegan parmesan, along with a charcuterie board with smoked salmon, salami, various cheeses, crackers, sliced baguette, honey, and apple slices."

"That's the first course?" Gabby blinked.

"Yes, ma'am. I'll also bring a Riesling from one of the top wineries in Washington." Tony walked away.

"I'm going to gain five pounds after today," she commented.

Sawyer sat back, his gaze scanning her body.

Her heart fluttered as heat filled her from head to toe and everything in between.

"I doubt it." He continued as he leaned closer. "We did a lot of walking today, plus you're totally sexy."

Her eyes crossed. "Sawyer..." she whispered.

"Tonight is a night for you to let go, Gabby." He took her left hand in his and raised it to his lips. "Tonight, I'm going to show you the sensual pleasure of food."

"And then?" Anticipation flowed through her.

"We'll see."

Chapter Three

♥

Sawyer loved the way Gabby enjoyed food. He'd make sure they would have a feast for breakfast tomorrow. He might be getting ahead of himself here, but he wanted Gabby in his bed tonight. They'd been flirting all day, and she wasn't immune to him.

While he'd never slept with a woman on the first date, Gabby made him want to break all his rules. She'd shown him how much today meant to her with her words and actions. No expectations that he should buy her things and even objecting to him spending so much on the tours he'd arranged.

"This must have cost a fortune," she said after the waiter removed their plates.

Was she reading his mind? "Nothing I couldn't handle."

"But..."

"No buts." He squeezed her shoulder and leaned closer. "The happiness on your face is worth it."

"Sawyer, that's so nice. It's just…" She waved her hand in the air. "Today has been wonderful, and I know there is more to come."

"There is. So put all thoughts about cost out of your head."

"It's hard."

"Why?" He was curious why she was constantly worried about money.

"It was the way I was brought up. We didn't have a lot, but we paid our own way."

"I understand. It can make it hard to accept letting someone else pay, but I want to do this." He'd never had to worry when he was growing up about where the next meal was coming from, or if his shoes needed replacing, or anything like that.

"My parents made it work, but there wasn't a lot for extra treats. I started working when I was fifteen to help out."

Sawyer frowned. "That's early." While he knew young people started working early, he hated it had happened to her.

"Even then, I knew I wanted to be a chef."

"What was your first job?"

"Washing dishes." She sighed. "It was a thankless job. While there were dishwasher machines, some of the pots had to be scrubbed by hand. But I learned a lot."

"I bet."

"The junior chef took pity on me and began showing me how to cook. That was fun." She grinned. "I learned a lot of swear words in that kitchen."

Sawyer almost spit out the water he'd sipped. "They taught you to swear?"

"Not really. There were some older male chefs, and they didn't always hold back when something went wrong or if customers sent their food back."

"I bet."

"Anyway, by the time I graduated college, I knew I wanted to be a chef. I was promoted to an assistant chef at the restaurant, and I went to culinary school."

"I bet that was expensive." He glanced up as Tony returned with their next course. The lobster rolls and Dungeness crab cakes were placed on the table, along with a new wine.

"The wine is a white burgundy that goes well with the lobster and crab," Tony said as he poured them each a glass. "Please enjoy."

"Lobster and crab?" Gabby stared at the plate.

"I figured it might be a good choice since you're from the Bay Area. Dungeness crab have a completely different taste than red or brown rock crab."

"I can't wait." She cut a piece of crab cake and ate it. "Goodness. These are delicious. The Old Bay seasoning isn't overwhelming, and the crab is so fresh."

Sawyer's pleasure skyrocketed at her words. He was ecstatic that she was happy and savoring the food. He took a bite of his own food. "It's perfect."

"Yes, it is. Anyway, back to your question. Culinary school was expensive, but I was lucky. I was able to get a couple grants, which covered most of the cost. The other chefs at the restaurant also chipped in by gifting me with little things."

"What kinds of little things?" He hated the idea that she might have struggled.

"The owner gave me a chef coat, apron, and hat. The executive chef gifted me with knives made for me and a sharpener. The rest of the staff chipped in and bought me basic utensils, a backpack, and a knife roll."

"That was generous of them."

"They were a good group. I worked with most of them throughout my schooling."

"How long did it take you?"

"About six years to get my bachelor's degree. I could only go to school part-time, but it did help that I was already working in a restaurant for my hands-on training." She took a bite of the lobster roll and let out a moan.

His dick hardened at the sound. Would she moan when they made love? He'd make sure of it. Sawyer took a sip of wine, willing his cock to calm down. The night was still young.

"How did you become a manager of a nightclub?"

Good question. "I was bored with my job in tech, so I was looking around for something new and found The Vault."

"You said you have an engineering degree, does that mean you also have some sort of technical degree?"

"Guilty."

"Heavy duty degrees."

"I was lucky. My parents were able to pay for my college." And then some. But he didn't add his thoughts. It wasn't time yet. He knew he'd have to tell her sooner or later, and it was selfish to wait, but he enjoyed being anonymous with Gabby and didn't want to ruin her night.

"Do you enjoy being a nightclub manager?"

"Most days." They'd finished their second course. The waiter cleared away the plates. "I like being around people and seeing that they're having fun. The paperwork, not so much."

"I hear you. Don't you have to work tonight?"

"The advantage..." He almost said, the advantage of being the owner. "Advantage of having another manager who can work so I could have the night off to spend with you."

Gabby gave him a small smile before she glanced out the window. "The view is beautiful."

The sun had begun to set, and the water gleamed as the lights around the city snapped on, making the city come alive. "I'm glad you're enjoying it."

"I am." She turned to him. Her eyes grew serious. "I don't like the idea of how much money you're spending on me."

They were back to that. "Gabby." He slipped closer as he squeezed her shoulder. "I wanted to do this. I'm not spending more than I can afford." Guilt filled him once again for hiding part of himself from her.

"Are you sure?" She sighed. "The tour this morning, this afternoon, lunch. Now this dinner and view." She waved her hand. "I'm sure a meal at the Space Needle isn't cheap."

"You're worth it." Her eyes widened at his words. "Has no one told you that before?"

She shook her head.

"Well, how short sighted of them. You are more than worth this dinner." He shifted in his seat. "I watched you today. In each store, you were respectful to the employees, patiently waited when you needed to. On the food tour, you always let the older couple go in front of us, and I saw you block that young couple from jumping in front of them at one point."

"That couple was rude. Always trying to be first." Her voice held a note of dislike.

"I noticed."

"I think others did, too, but I wasn't about to let them get away with it." She glanced at him. "Courtesy has become a lost art."

"I won't argue with that." There were fights at least once a week outside the club when the lines got too long, and it was obvious not everyone was going to get in. They'd taken to cutting the line off.

"I wish people would be better."

"You're an optimist." It was the first word that popped into his mind.

Gabby laughed. "Not always."

"No one is one hundred percent of something." He angled his head. "You can make me laugh and smile and not many people can do that." It was rare that anyone but Eric could do that.

"You've been around the wrong people."

Her words punched him in the gut. Outside of Eric, she was right. He rarely trusted anyone outside of his business partner, especially not a woman. With Gabby, it wasn't that way. He instinctively trusted her. He wasn't sure if that was good or not. "Maybe you're right."

The waiter returned with their main course. "Wagyu beef with potatoes and mixed vegetables." He placed the plates in front of them. "The wine pairing is a French Bordeaux." After pouring the wine, the server left.

"This beef smells heavenly," Gabby commented.

"It does." They ate without talking much. Sawyer's mind played with the possibilities of how tonight would end. Hopefully, in his apartment and bed, but he wouldn't push Gabby. It would be her choice.

By the time dessert was served, the sun had set. The lights of Seattle twinkled out the windows, making them seem like they were alone in the sky.

"Oh goodness." Gabby's voice was quiet.

The server had their dessert. A special one. Well, it was a pretty simple dessert, in his opinion. There was a big bowl filled with dry ice, and the dessert was sitting on top of the ice. When the waiter poured water over the dry ice, white smoke fanned out.

The first dessert was placed in front of her, then him. "Anything to drink?" the waiter asked.

"Coffee, please," Sawyer said.

"That sounds good." Gabby's eyes were fixed on the dessert, watching the smoke dissipate to reveal the contents of the dessert.

"Very good." The server walked away.

"I love how they did that." She picked up her spoon.

"I thought you might." Gabby might be a little burned out with her job, but she still enjoyed food and how it was presented.

By the time they finished dessert and their coffee, it was almost ten. Sawyer texted his driver, and they made their way downstairs. Gabby shivered as they walked outside. After sunset, the air had turned cooler.

"I left my jacket in the car," she said.

"I should have reminded you to grab it, but I'll keep you warm." He gathered her into his arms. "Better?"

"Yes." She snuggled against his chest. "This has been a wonderful day. I don't want it to end."

"It doesn't have to," he said softly. Gabby tilted her head back and looked up at him. No risk, no gain. "Come back to my place."

"I..." Her voice trailed off.

"No pressure. You don't have to."

"I know. You've been fantastic all day." She paused. "It isn't that I don't want to spend more time with you."

"Too soon."

"Maybe."

***

The second the word *maybe* left her lips, Gabby knew she wasn't telling the truth. She wanted to spend the night with Sawyer, but something held her back: Her own fear. Was she enough for a man like Sawyer? Her ex certainly didn't think she was much of a woman.

Rolling her eyes, she pushed all thoughts of her ex out of her mind and pushed out a breath. Here in Sawyer's arms, she felt safe. How often had that happened to her? Not since she was a child.

Lindsay's insistence to "let go" and "have fun" spun around in her mind. Three years of responsibility fell away. She wanted one night for herself. She wanted to be totally selfish and only think about herself.

"Let's go to your place."

His face registered surprise. "Are you sure?"

"Yes."

"If you want to go home, all you have to do is tell me."

"I will, but I'd like to see where you live."

His face froze.

"Unless you don't want to share with me?" She wouldn't push him.

"No, it's not that." The car pulled up, and Sawyer opened the door for her. He told the driver to go to home.

"I want to show you." Sawyer leaned down. "Again, no pressure. But I won't lie; I want to spend the night with you."

"I'd like that too." For once, Gabby was going to let go of all her fears, her worries, everything, and spend the night with this man who'd captured her attention. Hell, it probably wouldn't take much to capture her heart.

"I'm glad." He brushed a kiss over her lips. "I'll take this as slow or as fast as you want it."

"I appreciate that." She did. They'd only had soft, short kisses and light touches. Lord, this was so not like her. But she was attracted to Sawyer. Actually, it was more than attraction, maybe she was in lust with him.

Gabby wasn't thrilled with being in lust, yet she couldn't say she wasn't. Sawyer made her feel special, like a woman deserving of his attention. Several minutes later, they pulled up to a high-rise building.

"This is close to your club," she said, noting the neigh-borhood.

"Yes. I can walk to work." He helped her from the car, told the driver good night, and keeping his arm around her waist, guided her inside the building.

The lobby was tastefully decorated with sofas and chairs scattered around. There was a big reception desk with two men in uniforms seated behind it.

"Good evening, Mr. York," one of the men said.

"Good evening." He guided her to the elevators. Once inside, he slipped a card key into the slot and the pressed the button for the twenty-fifth floor.

"Security guards." She'd heard about buildings that had them but had never been in one.

"Yes. It's part of the amenities."

"And what are the other amenities?"

"Gym, roof top area for parties and other gatherings, conference rooms, housekeeping, things like that."

The casual way he said it made her wonder if Sawyer was used to this type of living. Maybe they needed to talk a bit more before she slept with him. Gabby inhaled sharply. Was she going to have sex with Sawyer? It was a possibility; otherwise, she wouldn't have come to his place.

The elevator doors opened into a nice foyer, with a door in front of them. She glanced around. Sawyer opened the only door and gestured for her to go in. Gabby froze inside the doorway. This wasn't any apartment or condo, but a penthouse.

"How do you afford this?"

"It's a perk from the owner of the club."

Gabby breathed a little easier. In her marriage, she'd seen how money inequity could change a person, and she didn't want to go through that again.

Sawyer took off his shoes and placed them in the wooden shoe rack. Gabby followed his lead, and he urged her forward into the living room.

The floor to ceiling windows framed the views of the waterfront and the Puget Sound. She automatically moved to them and stared. This place was high enough to have almost an unrestricted view.

"Would you like something to drink?" Sawyer moved across the room. "I have wine, beer, water, soda, coffee, or tea."

Her nerves danced beneath her skin. "Do you have a Riesling or Moscato?"

"Riesling, it is." He moved behind the bar.

Gabby tried to calm her nerves. It wasn't like she hadn't been with a man before, she had, just not in a while.

"Here you go." He held out a glass of wine to her.

"Thanks."

"Come sit down and relax." He gestured to the light gray sectional.

"What makes you think I'm not relaxed?" She made her way across the room and sat before she stared at him.

"Your muscles are tense." Sawyer took a seat but left room between their bodies. "Nothing will happen that you don't want to happen. I promise."

She released the breath she hadn't realized she was holding. "It's been a while for me."

"I mean what I said, Gabby. The night is in your hands."

"Okay." She forced herself to sit back against the sofa cushions. "Tell me more about how your boss gave you this penthouse as a perk."

***

Sawyer almost grimaced at Gabby's request. He hated lying to her, and he would stick to the truth as much as he could. "My boss has investment property all around Washington. He likes having his employees close and offered it to me." Partially the truth. He did have a lot of investment property.

"It's a great place."

"Where are my manners, do you want a tour?"

"I'm good." She sipped her wine. "Do you like living here?"

"Yes." He set his wine down. "The place has everything a person could want."

"What about companionship?"

"That is something they would have a hard time providing."

Gabby set her wine glass down and slid closer to him. "Maybe we can do something about that."

Sawyer slipped his arm around her shoulders, and she rested her head against him. "Are you lonely, Gabby?" He kept his voice soft.

"No...Yes...Probably." She laughed. "I want to be honest. I haven't been with a man since my ex."

He tensed up in shock, and immediately tried to relax so as not to alarm Gabby.

"Shocking, I know," she said.

Okay, he didn't manage to hide his surprise. "Why not? You were separated." He was curious.

"It didn't seem right." She shrugged. "I mean, my parents may not have had money, but they had each other. They supported each other no matter what."

"They sound like loving parents." While he knew his parents loved him, they weren't very demonstrative about it.

"They are. They're proud of what I've become."

"Lucky you." His father looked down at him for owning a nightclub, telling him he needed to go back to tech. Sawyer had been more than glad to get out of that corporate cutthroat world. "Tell me more about the executive chef world. How competitive is it?"

"It depends."

She snuggled deeper against his side, a good sign in his book.

"I was lucky. While the restaurant I work at is fairly elite, the staff are pretty down to earth."

"Did you have to fight for your job?" After all she'd gone to school for, it didn't seem fair if she had.

"Not really. The head chef liked me. Actually, all of the back of house, as I told you, was very supportive."

"Was there an executive chef?"

"Yes." She tilted her head back and grinned. "Carson was a great guy, an older gentleman who'd worked in the restaurant from day one. When I finished up my schooling and started moving my way up, he took me aside and told me he was retiring, and he wanted me to become executive chef."

"Was the head chef upset?" Sawyer had done a tiny bit of research so he'd understand how his kitchen would be run.

"No. He didn't want to be executive chef and told me to go for it. I understand more now."

"In what way?" Minute by minute, Gabby was melting against him. Talking was a good thing, especially since the topic wasn't him.

"Like I told you last night, the job requires a sixteen-hour day, almost seven days a week. While the pay is good, I'm starting to burn out."

"I get that." Wasn't that why he sold his tech company? Burnout and all the backstabbing.

"I enjoy being a chef and some of the aspects of my job."

"What else would you do?" He wanted to know about her dreams.

"Not sure. I've been thinking maybe a personal chef or maybe open a small café that didn't require a big staff. It's all up in the air."

"You'll figure it out."

"You sound so sure."

"I am." He was. In his short time with Gabby, he could tell she had drive and integrity. "You're a special woman."

Gabby leaned up and kissed his cheek. "You're special, too, Sawyer."

Unable to help himself, he turned his head, and their lips met. The kiss started off soft, his lips touching hers, backing away only to go back. She shifted, and her lips parted. Sawyer deepened the kiss.

The slow kiss turned into a passionate embrace. His tongue tangled with hers. He shifted, and Gabby was half lying down on the sofa with him over her. The kiss continued, and her hands slid around his neck, fingers playing with his hair.

Sawyer drew back and gazed down at Gabby. Her face was slightly flushed, her breathing rapid. Her green eyes were bright with desire. He lowered his head. He had no idea how much time they'd spent kissing and touching on the sofa.

"Shall we move this into the bedroom?" he asked, noticing her shirt was off, as was his.

"Yes."

He grinned as he stood, and swooped her into his arms.

"Sawyer!" She grabbed his shoulder.

"I won't drop you."

"I didn't think you would. It just startled me."

He strode down the hall to his bedroom. Thank goodness he'd left the lamp on so the room wasn't completely dark.

"This is a huge room." Her head moved from side to side, taking in the space.

"More room to ravish you." Sawyer placed her gently on her feet. While she continued to look around, he pulled back the covers.

"This is a nice bedroom, not too masculine but not too feminine."

"Bathroom's over there." He pointed to the half open door across the room as he stepped up to Gabby and ran his finger over her lace covered breasts.

"When did I lose my shirt?" Her gaze settled on his bare chest. "When did you lose yours?"

"I think we got carried away on the sofa." He traced the upper curve of her breasts.

"Somehow I don't mind." Her warm palms pressed against his pecs, and Sawyer could swear heat seared his skin.

"I'm glad." His fingers skimmed down to the fastening of her pants. Their gazes caught. "May I?" He tapped the material.

He caught the desire in her gaze as he followed the movement of her throat when she swallowed. "Yes, please."

His ego and his cock swelled. Even as the lust coursed though him, it brought with it a fierce need to take care of her for all time.

Sawyer undid the snap and lowered the zipper on her jeans. He cupped her hips before he slid the fabric down her toned legs. A shiver shook her as he stroked her calves with the lightest touch.

"Hold on to my shoulders," he said. When she complied, he lifted her right foot, pulled the jeans and her sock off, and did the same with the left. He pushed them aside and rose. "Beautiful."

A flush worked its way from her chest to her face. "I'm okay."

Sawyer tapped her lips with his finger. "Beautiful."

Gabby didn't say anything. "Your turn." Her fingers dipped inside his pants.

His cock was pressing against the fabric.

"Someone is…" She glanced up at him, her expression filled with mischief. "Big."

His laughter filled the room. Sawyer couldn't help himself. That wasn't what he'd expected her to say. She lowered the zipper, her movements slow and deliberate, and slid his trousers down. He stepped out of them.

He helped Gabby stand, pulled her into his arms, and took her lips with his. She leaned into him and kissed him with passion that took his breath away. His hands roamed over her back, to her ass, cupped it, and pulled her against his cock.

Her fingers dug into his shoulders as he continued to kiss her. He couldn't get enough of this woman. When they broke apart, their harsh breathing filled the air.

"I'm going to finish undressing you now."

She nodded.

Within a minute, she was naked in front of him. His eyes took in her full breasts, curvy hips, and long, toned legs. He lifted her and placed her on the bed. He couldn't wait to taste her. Climbing on the mattress, he pushed her legs apart.

"Sawyer." Uncertainty tinged her voice.

He lifted his gaze. "What is it, my sweet?"

She shifted. "Ummm..." Her flush deepened. "What are you doing?"

Shock went through him. "Sweetie, have you never had a man go down on you before?"

She shook her head.

"That ex of yours was an idiot." Sawyer couldn't believe her ex had never taken care of her this way. "Just relax."

"But..."

He tapped her mound with two fingers, not hard, but enough to get her attention. "There is no but. I'm going to take care of you now." Pushing her legs farther apart, he wiggled until his shoulders held her legs open.

Sawyer parted her labia. Her sweet scent filled him as he inhaled. "Pretty pussy." He ran his tongue over her.

Gabby squirmed.

"Stop moving."

"You have to be kidding."

He grinned before he licked her again.

***

Gabby wanted to fly off the bed. No man had ever gone down on her before. Sawyer's shock at that was surprising. Did men really like to do that to women? Not in her experience. But damn, Sawyer ran his tongue over her slit like he was licking an ice cream cone.

She had no idea how to react. It was hard to hold still and not squirm. Did she smell down there? She'd taken a shower this morning, but they'd walked around all day. Her nerves kicked up a notch.

"You're so tense."

"No kidding."

"Hey, what's going on?" He maneuvered his body until he was lying on his side next to her, with his head propped up on his hand.

How did she explain it? Gabby closed her eyes. "I..." The words wouldn't come.

"Sweetheart." He caressed her cheek with a tender touch, and she opened her eyes. Sawyer was staring down at her with concern and worry in his eyes.

Her heart tightened. "It's not you." Those words sounded lame.

"What is it?" He leaned over and kissed her collarbone. "Did you not like me tasting you?"

She wanted to say yes but couldn't. "That didn't bother me."

"Is it because no man has ever licked you before?"

"Partially." Lord, this was embarrassing. Why couldn't Sawyer be more like her ex and just do a quickie?

"Talk to me, please."

The please tugged at her heart. "It's going to sound silly."

He nipped at her chin before staring into her eyes. "Nothing sounds silly."

Taking a shaky breath, she gathered her courage. "I was worried about how I smelled down there."

Sawyer blinked. "You smell delicious."

He didn't think she was silly or crazy or anything else. "I do?"

"Gabby, women have their own unique scent. Yours to me is..." He paused. "I'm trying to find the right words. You smell like summer, fresh, clean, and ready to play."

Her heart lightened. "Really?"

"Yes. I don't lie." His mouth brushed against her. "Maybe we leave that for later."

His palm covered her left breast and squeezed.

Gabby's breath rushed out of her when he did the same to the right.

"At least I know I turn you on."

"Any more on and I'd light up Seattle."

Sawyer chuckled. "Let me see if we can do that."

He leaned over and licked one nipple and then the other. Gabby moaned as tingles flowed through her body. How had she not known how this would feel?

Her fingers curved around his shoulders. Sawyer was so strong yet so gentle with her. Not that she minded his gentleness, but she wanted more.

"More," she whispered.

Sawyer's gaze burned into her as his hand wandered over her stomach to her mound. One finger parted her pussy lips. "Don't you like foreplay?"

"I've never had an opportunity to find out."

He shook his head. "Let me show you."

Gabby thought she would die from pleasure as Sawyer explored every inch of her body with his hands, lips, and tongue. "Please."

Sawyer paused; the heat in his gaze had her squirming on the bed. He reached over, grabbed a condom, and slipped it on. His eyes locked with hers, and he pushed into her pussy.

A groan escaped Gabby as he filled her. It had been a while, and Sawyer wasn't a small man. But the slight burn and stretching sensation brought her to life. She hadn't felt this way in a long time, if ever.

"Sweetheart, I'm not going to last long if you keep clenching my dick."

"Feels so good."

"It should." He slid out and back in, slowly building the pace.

Gabby's nails dug into his back as he made love to her. Slow and steady until she was ready to cry out in frustration. He finally picked up the pace, and she loved it. He felt so good inside her.

Her toes tingled, and her stomach quivered. She wasn't going to last long, but it didn't matter to her. This man took her to the brink of a climax.

Her body shuddered. "I'm..." She never got the words out. Her body exploded like a pressure cooker. Her pussy clenched around his cock, and tears leaked from the corners of her eyes. Sawyer continued to thrust, finally giving one last thrust, and his cock pulsed.

He kept his weight off of her as her body stopped shaking. His lips captured hers, but she had to break away to breathe.

"Gabby?" His voice was soft and gentle. "Sweetheart, did I hurt you?"

"No," she whispered as she sniffled, her eyes tightly closed. She couldn't look at him. How could she possibly explain? It all had to do with Sawyer. This man pampered her today, listened to her, and made sure she was happy. She'd never known happiness like this.

"You're crying." He pulled back, and she heard him moving before his arms came around her, and he pulled her against him. "What's wrong?"

"Nothing." No matter what she did, she couldn't stop the tears.

"There must be something." His arms tightened around her.

Her head rested on his chest, and her tears continued. How could she explain it to him? She had to find a way. "You did nothing wrong."

"The jury is out on that." Soft tissues touched her face.

Gabby lifted her head and opened her eyes. Sawyer's face was filled with concern, and that almost started more tears. He lifted his hand and wiped the tears away from her face with a gentle touch.

"I got you wet." Her voice was a bit wobbly.

"I'll dry." He tossed the used tissues on the nightstand.

"I meant what I said, Sawyer. You did nothing wrong. I was overwhelmed by emotion." His features softened. "I've never...what I'm trying to say is, it's rare that a man can make me climax without playing with my clit." There, she said it. She only hoped he didn't think she was defective.

"Oh, Gabby." His palm cupped her cheek. "Not all women can climax from penetration. I'm glad I could do that for you."

She blinked. "Who are you?" He understood and didn't get upset. How had she found a man like him?

Sawyer laughed. "I'll admit I'm not your average man, but I do understand a woman's body."

"Thank god for that." Gabby laid her head back on his damp chest. They laid there in a comfortable silence.

***

Sawyer barely stopped himself from swearing out loud. Gabby's ex was an ass. Sawyer was sure he was the one who'd made Gabby doubt herself. She'd opened herself to him and been brave enough to tell him something so personal. This woman kept surprising him.

He held her close to his body as she continued to come down from her climax but also to absorb her feelings and calm down himself. He'd jumped to the wrong conclusion when Gabby started crying, thinking he was at fault. After she'd explained, he'd relaxed, body and soul.

He'd give her time to recover, and he'd show her again how she should be worshipped. Right now, he was happy with her in his arms.

Chapter Four

♥

Sawyer lay there, holding Gabby against his chest. She'd fallen asleep after their third lovemaking session. Her reactions to him had been pure and genuine. Unlike other women he'd known. Damn, he was jaded. Maybe he'd been around all the wrong type of women.

Gabby shifted, and he tightened his arms around her. He didn't want to let her go. Ever. The thought shocked him. It wasn't like him to get this attached to someone so quickly. Gabby had broken the mold.

He closed his eyes, enjoying the slight weight of her against his body. His mind was already planning Sunday morning breakfast. He was trying to impress her with food, but he also recognized he had to be careful.

She was already suspicious of the money he'd spent on her. He could try and cook breakfast tomorrow, but that wasn't a good idea. He didn't cook much, and he wanted to give her more than toast and coffee. He'd order from his favorite place.

Since it was Sunday, they could spend the day at his place. He wanted to show Gabby there was more to him than sex and food.

His gut tightened. He hadn't told her the truth about his money. Maybe tomorrow he would. But he didn't want to ruin today. If they decided to continue to date after she went back to the Bay Area, he'd tell her more. Sawyer already knew he wanted Gabby in his life. Now all he needed to do was convince her.

***

Gabby woke to the smell of coffee.

"Wake up, sleepy head."

She opened her eyes to see Sawyer sitting on the bed, holding a mug, his hip next to hers.

"What time is it?" Even her voice was groggy.

"A little after ten."

Ten? She never slept this late. Gabby sat up and grabbed the sheet to cover her nudity while heat flooded her body.

"I'll leave this on the nightstand. You'll find a fresh toothbrush in the bathroom, along with towels." He set the mug on the table and stood. "Breakfast will be ready in thirty minutes, is that enough time."

"Yes. Thank you."

Sawyer shook his head, and leaned down and kissed what sense she still had right out of her. Forgetting to hold on to the sheet, she entwined her arms around his neck. He snagged her arms and lowered them.

"As much as I'd love to crawl back into that bed with you and ravish you all over again, you need food." He flicked his finger over her taut nipple. "Thirty minutes." Sawyer turned and sauntered out of the room.

Gabby watched him, noticing how his gait wasn't as steady as it usually was, and damn if he didn't have muscles rippling over his back. She itched to jump out of bed and run her palms over his tan skin.

When he was out of her sight, Gabby shook her head and took a sip of coffee. Perfect. How did he know? Oh, from dinner last night. He paid attention to how much milk and sugar she put into her coffee.

Observant man. What else had he noticed? Cradling the mug in one hand, she climbed out of bed and made her way into the bathroom. Her mouth dropped open. She could fit her whole apartment in here. Beautiful mosaic tile, a huge shower with a garden tub next to it.

Glancing at the sink, she caught her reflection in the mirror. "Oh dear God." The words slipped from her lips.

Her hair was all over the place, any make-up she had on last night was gone. Thank goodness for smudge proof mascara. Ugh. She breathed into her hand. Morning breath. And still, Sawyer had kissed her and looked at her like she was the most beautiful thing in the world.

Her stomach flipped over. She'd never been around a man like Sawyer, and she wasn't sure how to handle him. She giggled. Oh she handled him all right last night. Taking a long drink of her coffee, she set the mug on the counter. She twisted her hair up so it wouldn't get wet and stepped into the shower.

She turned on the water and flipped the shower on. She jumped as the cool water hit her skin, but it soon warmed up. Okay, first things first. A quick shower, brush teeth, and get... Clothes?

Gabby didn't have any clothes. She hadn't even bothered to look for what she wore yesterday. Well, damn what was she going to do? Quickly, she washed up and wrapped her body in a towel.

After brushing her teeth, and using a comb left on the counter for her hair, she glanced around the bathroom. There was a robe on the back of the door. Probably Sawyers'. Well, it was better than a towel. Although walking into the kitchen with just a towel on did give her some pleasurable ideas. Food first, though.

She slipped the soft mauve material on. It was velvety against her skin, reminding her of the way Sawyer caressed her last night. His hands had roamed every inch of her body. A flash of heat went through her. With a deep breath, she pushed away the memories of last night and hung the damp towel over the hamper, grabbed her empty cup, and ventured out.

She stopped when she saw her clothes neatly folded on the bed. Her underwear sat on top, and heat filled her. Gabby picked up her panties. Thank goodness her clothes were wash and wear material. The underwear was still warm. It hit her. He'd thrown her clothes in the washer and dryer.

This man continued to surprise her. Slipping off the robe, she dressed quickly and made her way out of the bedroom and down the hallway. She could hear Sawyer in the kitchen and stopped in her tracks when she entered the living room. The view was stunning. It had been last night, but in the light of day... The natural light into the room made everything seem bright and airy.

"Hungry?" Sawyer asked.

Her stomach growled. "Yes." Surprisingly, she was. "I hope you don't mind. I borrowed your robe." Her gaze took in the lowriding sweats and t-shirt he wore. Gabby's palms itched to touch his solid chest.

His eyes darkened. "I bet it looked a lot better on you than me."

"You flatter me."

"Go sit down. I'll bring the food." He gestured to the dining room table. Gabby did as he requested. The table was already set.

"I love this view," she said as she sat down. Gabby never realized what great views of the sound and mountains these apartments had.

Sawyer walked in with several platters, put them on the table, and left. Her eyes widened. Pancakes, eggs, bacon, sausage, and waffles. Was he feeding an army? When Sawyer came back, he had a cheese and fruit platter, along with a carafe of coffee and orange juice.

"Are you expecting company?" she asked.

"No. Why?" He took a seat next to her. His body heat called out to her.

"I can't believe you'd cook all this for the two of us." She gestured to the food laden table.

He glanced at the table. "I did go overboard, didn't I. Sometimes, I order more than is needed." His eyes twinkled. "I'm not a very good cook."

"Trying to impress a chef?"

"If I say yes, would that earn me a kiss."

"You'll get one anyway." Gabby leaned over and brushed a kiss over his lips. "Where do I start?" She looked over the food. It all looked so good. She took a pancake, waffle, several pieces of bacon and sausage. That would be a good start.

"What would you like to do today?" Sawyer asked as he filled his plate.

Gabby stared at him. "I probably should spend some time with Lindsay."

"I get that. After breakfast, give her a call or a text and see what she'd like to do today. I'm game for anything."

Gabby tilted her head. "You don't have to do this."

"I know I don't. I want to."

She shook her head.

"What?" he asked.

"You're too good to be true." She returned to her breakfast.

"What do you mean?" he asked after a few minutes.

"I mean..." Gabby waved her fork in the air. "Making yesterday so special. That must have cost a fortune and was more than enough."

"Still doesn't answer my question."

She nibbled at a piece of bacon, trying to think of how to say what was in her mind. "Don't take this the wrong way. You're a great guy. Any woman would be happy to have your attention."

"But you don't."

"That's not what I meant." Why was this so hard for her? Maybe because she never liked talking about money. "Sawyer, I told you about how I grew up."

He nodded.

"I've always been careful about money, only buying what is necessary with occasional treats. The money you spent yesterday is probably more than I spend in a several years on fun stuff."

"Can you tell me why it bothers you so much that I spent money on you?"

She shook her head.

"Gabby, I want to understand. I asked you if I could show you Seattle, and you agreed."

"I did, but I didn't expect—" She waved her hands in the air. "Everything. I've thought about it. Dinner alone had to be at least five hundred dollars. That's a fortune."

Why did he look away every time she said that word? Sawyer pushed his half-eaten food away. "Maybe, but I wanted to do it."

"I know, and I'm grateful."

"I didn't do it for gratitude or even to get you to spend the night with me. I did it because I wanted to. Because

I like you and wanted to spend time with you. Besides, you deserve some pampering." Sawyer stood up and began pacing in front of the window.

"I'm not sure why you think that."

He faced her. His body tense and his eyes flaming. "What did that ex-husband of yours tell you?"

Gabby squirmed and pushed her chair back.

Sawyer walked over to her, turned her chair to the side, and knelt down in front of her. His hands took hers. "Sweetheart, tell me."

She could barely breathe. Sawyer did that to her. Took her breath away. Here was this powerful man, kneeling in front of her, trying to understand her feelings around money. "My ex encouraged me to become an executive chef."

"But?"

Might as well get it out. "He spent the money I earned as fast as I earned it." Sawyer cursed, and her shoulders relaxed. "Part of me knew what he was doing, so I started keeping money back, but I should have stopped it."

"Dare I ask what he spent it on?"

"Video games and such. New TVs, new gaming systems, things I really didn't pay attention to like I should have."

"It took me months to realize our joint checking account barely had a balance when it should have had a very healthy amount."

"What did you do?" His fingers tightened around his.

"Confronted him. He made all sorts of excuses, and after that, I made sure to put only a small amount in the joint account."

"You did the right thing."

"I like to think so. He did try to get into my private account."

"Ass."

"Yeah. The bank wouldn't let him access the account, thank goodness." When the bank called her all those years ago, her heart had frozen. Luckily, they denied him access, and her money was safe. Of course they had a big fight about it when she got home from work that night. That's when she told him she wanted a divorce. Gabby blew out a breath. "Believe it or not, we had a pre-nup that kept our assets separate. So, when we divorced, I was able to keep everything that was mine."

"Thank goodness. Not everyone wants a pre-nup."

"At the time, I thought it was a bit silly, but later, I was so grateful." Lindsay was the one who'd suggested it. She had a sixth sense about those things.

"I remember you said your ex dragged his feet in the divorce."

"Yes." She tugged at her hands. "If we're going to talk about it, let's be a bit more comfortable and get you off your knees."

Sawyer grinned. "You got it." He stood, pulled her to her feet, and guided her over to the sofa.

Gabby sagged against the sofa, allowing it to encase her body. "My ex didn't want to divorce me because he thought he'd continue to get money from me." There, she said it.

"Alimony?"

"Probably, he figured if he never answered the divorce paperwork or anything else my lawyer sent to him, I'd continue to pay for things."

"But you didn't."

"No. While lawyers are not cheap, I had a really good one. Even the judge was good. Oh, my ex would answer one or two little things to look like he was responding." Gabby shifted toward Sawyer. "I asked the court to grant me the right not to support a man I was not living with and who was able to work. The judge granted it."

"How long did that take?"

"Six months after I moved out. Quick for California courts."

"Last night you were celebrating your divorce. How long did that take?"

"Almost three years." She sighed. "Like I said, he'd respond just enough to keep the court happy."

"How did you finally get him to agree?"

"I didn't. I was lucky. My lawyer found a loophole, and he got me a default judgment for divorce due to my ex's nonresponse."

"That was lucky."

"In a way, it was. I call it a loophole, but there is an actual statute. I don't fully understand it all, but it's finally over."

"I am too. And it does help me understand why you're sensitive to me spending money."

"Thank you. It's hard. Even having Lindsay pick up the bill Friday night made me cringe."

Sawyer nodded. "So, we're back to the beginning of this conversation. What would you like to do today?"

"First, I think we need to clear away breakfast and do the dishes."

"So practical." He pushed up from the sofa.

"Yes." Gabby stood. "I'll text Lindsay and see if she wants to do anything. If she's fine at home, I might be able to be talked into a movie."

"Now that will be fun."

***

Sawyer helped Gabby clear the table, but his mind was elsewhere. She didn't know he'd partially picked up the tab Friday night. He only charged Lindsay for the food, not the alcohol. And how much he spent yesterday.

He understood better why she worried about him spending money. She had no clue who he really was. Guilt settled like a lead ball in his gut. He wanted to tell her, but feared she'd walk away. Sawyer shook his head. He wasn't ready for that, and he wondered now if he ever would be.

She was going to walk away anyhow. Gabby had a job back in the Bay Area. She wouldn't stay in Seattle, even if he wanted her to. Maybe her not staying was a good thing—less worry for him. But a part of him didn't want her to go back.

Love at first sight didn't exist, but he wanted to keep her close to him. Last night had been wonderful, and he wanted more nights like that with her. Damn it all, he didn't know how to make this work. Another first for him. He usually knew how to solve any problem.

"You're staring at that dish like it's your mortal enemy," Gabby said with laughter in her voice.

"Huh?" Sawyer dragged his gaze from the platter on the table. "I was lost in thought." He picked up the platters and carried them into the kitchen.

"That was obvious." Gabby began loading the dishwasher.

"You don't need to do that."

"I don't mind."

Those three little words had Sawyer taking a deep breath. It was obvious to him now he'd been dating the wrong women. Probably because those were the crowds he hung around with when he was in the tech world.

Even with the nightclub, he was still involved with the movers and shakers in Seattle. He thought maybe he'd get away from them, but they still sought him out.

Gabby would easily hold her own with Seattle's elite, yet she was comfortable putting the dishes in the dishwasher. Women in his past would turn their noses up at such menial tasks. She enjoyed walking around Pike Place Market, exploring the underground of Seattle. Her pure appreciation of the food at the Space Needle. Her moans of pleasure last night. She wasn't putting on an act. This was the real Gabby. How could he convince her to move to Seattle? Was it even possible? Sawyer wasn't one to give up easily. He'd feel her out this afternoon. They needed more time to explore their relationship.

"What movie would you like to watch?" he asked once they were back in the living room.

"I love action/adventure, but also really cheesy disaster movies." She grinned. "Wait. Where's your TV?"

Sawyer picked up the remote, hit the button, and the TV rose from the white cabinet across the room.

"That's clever." She paused for a moment. "And big."

"It's only seventy inches."

"Only." Gabby giggled. "Men and their toys."

"I haven't shown you all my toys yet."

"Oh?" Gabby snuggled up to him as he found an old disaster movie about earthquakes in California.

"Are you tempting me?" Sawyer slid his arm around her shoulders, enjoying the feel of her body against his. He could get used to this.

"Later. This is my favorite."

***

Gabby kept her gaze on the TV screen when all she wanted to do was gaze up at Sawyer's handsome face. This man kept her body humming and her mind happy. Funny how that had happened so quickly.

It hadn't been easy for her to share her marriage failure, but Sawyer hadn't judged her or made her feel stupid.

He seemed to understand, and that made her like him even more. Heck, who was she kidding, she was already half-way in love with him.

It was too quick. People didn't fall in love in thirty-six hours. Especially since her divorce was just finalized five days ago. Lindsay would tell her she was being silly. Her marriage had been over for three years.

What was she going to do? He lived in Seattle. She lived in the Bay Area. It's not like she hadn't been thinking of moving; she had. While she loved her job, it was beginning to be a grind. With her divorce and the money she'd saved, she'd been thinking about opening her own little bakery/café.

She couldn't do that in the Bay Area; prices alone would drive her out of business. But could she do it in Seattle? Maybe not the city proper but outside of it? She needed to do more research and figure it all out.

Opening a bakery, any business really, was a risk. Plus, she had no idea of the hoops she might need to jump through. Sawyer might be able to help her there. After all, he managed the nightclub. He'd have some idea of the requirements.

"How long have you managed The Vault?"

Surprise flittered across his face. "Since it opened five years ago."

"You were in on the ground floor."

"Yep."

"Was it difficult to open?"

Sawyer shifted but didn't move her from where she rested her head right below his shoulder on his chest. "Paperwork galore. Actually, there's still paperwork galore. Seattle has some very strict rules."

"I noticed you had five bouncers, one at the VIP door, two at the regular door, and two monitoring the lines."

"We've had some issues with fights in line, so I have the bouncers there especially once we close them. We card everyone coming in."

"I experienced that." She had wondered about the requirement.

"This way, we keep minors out."

"The Vault is twenty-one and over?"

"It was easier since we're serving alcohol."

Gabby nodded. She enjoyed being snuggled against Sawyer. It made her feel safe and secure.

"There are always inspections, both for the food and alcohol," he continued. "They also make sure the building is up to code and in compliance with fire regulations."

"I hadn't thought about that." Maybe she should go to work at an established place first. But she wasn't sure that's what she wanted.

"Why the questions?"

She bit her lip. Would he think her idea crazy? "I was curious." This wasn't the time or place to discuss her plans in detail. She tried to concentrate on the movie but couldn't. Now that the idea had taken root, she wanted to explore it more.

Lindsay would be a great person to bounce this all off of. Her friend had lived here long enough to know which areas would be good and which wouldn't. How large a place would she need? How much staff? Her mind was running away with thoughts and plans.

"Are you okay?" Sawyer asked.

Gabby blinked. "Fine. Why?"

"The movie is over, and you haven't moved."

"Oops." Her cheeks heated. "I was a little lost in thought."

"What else would you like to do?"

As much as Gabby wanted to stay and snuggle with Sawyer, she couldn't. "I really should get back to Lindsay's place."

"I see."

Coldness seeped from him making her shiver. "Don't be upset. I ditched her all day yesterday and part of today."

"I get it." He removed his arm, and Gabby sat up.

Gabby was at a loss, so she let her heart speak for her. "I don't want to leave, Sawyer, but it's not fair that I flew up here to celebrate with Lindsay, and I've left her alone."

He ran his hand through his hair. "You're right. Let me put some clothes on, and I'll get you back to her place."

"You can go as you are. I don't mind."

His gaze heated. "The more clothing between us the better. Trust me." He walked into the bedroom.

She sighed, knowing he was right. But she really wanted to ignore all her good sense and follow him into his bedroom.

Sawyer came back in jeans and a polo shirt, looking as delicious as he did in sweats and a t-shirt. Her gut tightened. This man had become so important to her in such a short period of time. It scared her.

"Ready?" he asked.

"As I'll ever be." She grabbed her purse and reached for her bags, but Sawyer got to them first.

"I'll carry them for you."

"Thank you."

The ride in the elevator was silent, and Gabby hated it. By voicing her need to get back to Lindsay, they'd become strangers. When the elevator doors opened, they were in a garage. She hadn't even thought about where he might park his vehicle.

With his free hand, Sawyer guided her to a sparkling dark blue SUV. It wasn't a road yacht; it was a smaller one. This was more what she expected from a nightclub manager. After putting her bags in the back, he held the passenger door open for her.

Gabby climbed in, enjoying the soft leather seats and ample leg room. She buckled her seatbelt as Sawyer got behind the wheel. She wanted to say something to him, but didn't know what.

He started the engine, and they were on their way. "Do you need directions?"

"No, I remember the way." He glanced over at her. "Unless you've changed your mind?"

She shook her head, not trusting herself to voice her willingness to go back to his apartment. Gabby stared out at the window. Yesterday and last night had been wonderful, even this morning. Now everything felt off to her. Tense and unyielding.

In no time at all, he pulled up in front of Lindsay's building, parked, and climbed out of the vehicle before she could say a word. Gabby opened her door and slid out as Sawyer grabbed her bags out from the trunk area.

"I can take those." She held out her hand.

"Not yet." He snagged her around the waist and pulled her close. "I'm going to miss you."

Tension seeped out of her body, and she relaxed against him. "Me too."

He gave a half grin before he lowered his head.

Their lips met, and the kissing dance began. Sawyer backed her up against his vehicle as the kiss went on and on. When he finally pulled back, Gabby stood there, eyes closed, lips slightly parted.

"Goodness." She wanted nothing more than to say the hell with it and pull him back into her arms for another kiss, but the rational part of her dissented.

"Why don't you and Lindsay come by the club tonight. I'll keep a table open for you."

"I'll talk to Lindsay." And she would. It couldn't be too late of a night because she did have to fly home tomorrow, but it wouldn't hurt to see Sawyer one more time.

"Good." He stepped away. Taking her hand, he led her to the entrance gate into Lindsay's apartment complex.

Gabby rang the bell. "Hello," Lindsay's voice sounded scratchy.

"Hey, Lindsay, it's me. Let me in."

"You got it." The line went dead, and the buzzer for the gate sounded.

Gabby pushed the gate open and turned to Sawyer. "I had a great time." She took her bags from him.

He nodded. "Tonight." Sawyer leaned down and pressed a hard kiss against her lips before he turned and went back to his vehicle.

She stepped through the gate and closed it. She stood there watching until the SUV pulled away. Her heart grew heavy as she made her way to Lindsay's apartment.

Her friend was standing with the door open, her expression a mixture of mischief and anticipation. "Tell me everything."

Chapter Five

♥

"Oh my goodness, girl. When I told you to go for it, I didn't expect this."

"I know." Gabby had gone through everything from her time with Sawyer, including them sleeping together.

"What has you spooked? Too soon after the divorce?"

"I wouldn't think so. I mean I've been separated for over three years, and I certainly didn't love my ex anymore. We'd grown so far apart."

"Yeah, he really only wanted your money."

"So true." Gabby shifted. "I think that's why I was bothered with Sawyer spending so much on me yesterday."

"It sounded like he wanted to. It wasn't like you asked him to do all those things for you."

"I know; it still bothers me though."

"I'd love to punch your ex. He did such a number on you."

"Probably. I don't know. Something with Sawyer didn't feel right."

"What?"

"It was much more than paying for stuff Saturday. It's the place he's living."

"I thought you said the apartment was a perk of his job."

"That's what Sawyer said." She rubbed her forehead. "Did you remember where you know him from?

Lindsay shook her head. "You don't believe him about the apartment?"

"I'm not sure." Her gut churned. "He's so comfortable there, like he's used to money. The place was pristine. At times, I was afraid I'd mess things up or break something."

"Did Sawyer seem at all concerned?"

"Not one bit."

"What else?"

"This morning when he brough me home, he drove a small but still luxury SUV, one I'm sure was at least sixty thousand dollars or more."

"Maybe it's a lease." Lindsay stared at her. "Quit looking for reasons to dislike Sawyer."

"That's the problem." Gabby rubbed between her breasts. "I'm falling for him."

"Way to go," Lindsay yelled. "Or is it?"

"I don't know. Part of me wonders if there's something I'm missing, some side of him that isn't the caring, wonderful man I spent yesterday with. The other part is telling me to just go with it."

"I say go with it."

"Of course you would." Gabby laughed. Was she being overly critical? Probably. She hated feeling this way. The past three years she'd mapped out her life and how easily she'd been thrown into turmoil. "Did I tell you Sawyer invited us to the club tonight?"

"What?" Lindsay's face lit up.

"Yes, he said he'd hold a table for us."

"Are we going?" Lindsay practically vibrated with excitement.

"I have a feeling you want to."

"Yes, please. Everyone at my job will be so jealous." Gabby chuckled.

"I'll even give you an mani-pedi if you say yes."

Now that was a deal Gabby would make. "We can go but not too late. I have to fly home tomorrow morning."

"Don't remind me."

"Lindsay?" Gabby hated the dismay in her friend's face.

"Why don't you move up here? You know you could get a job easily, and we'd be closer to each other."

"I've thought about it."

"Let me get everything set up, and we can talk as I work." Lindsay jumped off the sofa.

Gabby sat there, wondering. What was stopping her from moving here?

***

Three hours later, not only did Gabby have a mani-pedi, she and Lindsay had talked over the idea of Gabby moving here. Gabby had also done some research and applied for a couple of jobs.

"To make this work, I'd have to find a job first." Gabby noted where she'd applied on the list they'd pulled together. "And a place to live."

"You can stay with me until you find something you want."

"This will take some time. Finding a job and I have to give my notice and pack up my place."

"Once you have everything in place, I'll fly down and help you pack. Your apartment is so small, I'm sure there isn't that much."

That was true. Mainly her two bookcases full of books, her TV, clothes, kitchen stuff, and other nicknacks. The rest of the apartment furniture wasn't worth anything. She'd bought most of it second hand.

"I really need to think this through. I can't believe you talked me into applying for jobs already. This feels too fast."

"What is there to think about?"

"You know I'm not one to just jump into things." Well, most of the time anyway. But deep in her gut, she knew this was the right move.

"I know, but I think it's time for you to have a change. You need to get out of your rut."

"Am I in a rut?" Was she? It was possible. For the last three years she'd concentrated on her job and trying to get her divorce.

"You are. Tell you what, we've got a few hours until we can go to the Vault. You keep looking at job openings in the area, and I'll fix us something to eat."

Gabby nodded. "Nothing heavy."

"Salad it is."

Gabby opened up her internet browser on her phone and continued the job search.

***

Sawyer glanced at his watch again. It was only seven, and the doors to the Vault wouldn't open for another hour. He was impatient to see Gabby again.

"You reserved table one for your lady friend, I see," Eric said.

"Yes."

"It explains why you're acting like an alley cat."

"What?" Sawyer glared at his friend.

"All jumpy and anxious."

Sawyer couldn't deny Eric's words. He was. Gabby had been very quiet on the drive to Lindsay's place, but that kiss had been explosive. He hoped Gabby would show up tonight, and he could at least spend a little more time with her.

He hated she was flying back tomorrow, but he was determined to keep in contact with her. It wasn't like he couldn't fly down and see her. It might be difficult, and he'd owe Eric big time if he did it on weekends. Gabby was worth it.

"Excuse me." Jesse, one of the bartenders, stood by the stairs.

"What's up?" Jesse was the one who invited Lindsay and gave her the VIP table, and Sawyer was happy he had. That way he got to meet Gabby.

"Chef sent me up to get one of you. Apparently, there's an issue with the food for tonight."

"I'll go," Sawyer told Eric. It would keep his mind off the time.

***

An hour and half later, Sawyer made his way out of the kitchen. Someone had placed the boxes of chicken in the wrong fridge, and Chef was going nuts. It took Sawyer some time, but he found it tucked in a corner.

Now, Chef was happy, Sawyer walked out of the kitchen and to the bar. He glanced at table one, and his heart skipped a beat. Gabby was there. She and Lindsay were chatting. Their waiter, Brad, made his way to the table with food and drink.

A charcuterie board, fries, and what looked like margaritas. Nice. He waited until Brad walked away to make his way over to them.

"Good evening."

Gabby looked up. "Sawyer." Her voice was soft.

His heart lightened, and the night seemed better now that she was here.

"Thanks for the table and inviting us," Lindsay said.

"You're more than welcome." The DJ was playing a soft ballad since it was early. "Dance with me?" He extended his hand to Gabby.

She looked at her friend who smiled.

"Okay."

With her hand in his, he led her out onto the dance floor and pulled her into his arms. "I missed you this afternoon."

She laid her head on his collarbone. "I missed you too."

"What did you and Lindsay do?"

"Just girl stuff."

"Good." He really didn't want to question her. Sawyer kept her close as they swayed to the music, enjoying the feeling of her body against his. He wanted more of this. The song came to an end way too fast.

Sawyer was going to continue dancing into the next song when he glanced up and saw Eric motioning to him. He sighed. "Work calls." He led her back to her table and went to see what Eric wanted.

***

Gabby glanced at Lindsay, who was smiling from ear to ear. "We only danced," Gabby said.

"I know, but that man is so into you. Did you tell him about your plans?"

"No." It was too soon. She'd found a few job openings that sounded promising, but she couldn't commit to anything until she knew for sure she had a job.

"But—"

"Nothing," Gabby interrupted her friend. "There's still a lot to figure out. I'm not going to rush into this."

"I hear you." Lindsay glanced toward the bar. "Is it okay if Jesse joins us on his break?"

"Sure. I've been curious about him."

"We're not dating or anything. It's just been casual meetups."

"Yeah, sure." Gabby knew her friend.

Ten minutes later, Jesse came to their table. Gabby moved so he could sit next to Lindsay. He gave Lindsay a kiss on the cheek and took her hand. "How are you ladies tonight?"

"We're good. Jesse, this is Gabby, my best friend."

"Hi, Gabby." Jesse smiled at her.

As they talked, she found out Jesse had been working at The Vault for the past three years, and he worked at a gym. Gabby found him to be a nice guy.

"I saw you dancing with the boss," he said.

"Sawyer?"

"Yes."

"Boss?" Gabby asked, and shook her head. "That's right. He's the manager here."

Jesse laughed. "He's so much more than the manager. Sawyer co-owns the club."

Gabby froze. "Co-owns?" Sawyer was a partner in the club, not just a manager?

"Yeah, Eric and Sawyer started The Vault five years ago."

Gabby's mouth dried out. The pieces started falling into place like a puzzle. Everything from yesterday flooded through her. The food tour, dinner at the Space Needle, the penthouse apartment. His penthouse. She'd bet everything she owned that he owned it.

Sawyer had lied to her and not just once. His job, where he lived. His familiarity with the driver had confused her. Now she knew. The driver, the car, they were his. And the club. He owned it.

"That's nice," Gabby said, trying to shake away her discovery. She didn't want to be rude to Jesse. He had no idea of the bombshell he'd dropped.

"Well, my break is over." He stood. "Lindsay, I'll call you next week." Jesse dropped a kiss on Lindsay's forehead and said goodbye.

"Gabby?" There was concern in Lindsay's voice.

"I need to go." Gabby couldn't stay here, not now. Sawyer had lied about everything, but especially, he lied about the one thing she never wanted to argue about again since her divorce. Money. She shivered as icy tendrils of betrayal flowed over her skin.

"What is going on?"

"Sawyer told us he managed the club, not that he owned it. He covered it up. Oh, God, I think I love him, and he lied to me."

"Oh, my God. It just hit me. I knew he looked familiar. If I'd remembered sooner, I'd have told you.

"I don't care." Gabby looked around in a panic. "I have to get out of here. I'll get a ride share."

"Nope." Lindsay grabbed her purse. "I'm going with you."

Together, they raced out after Lindsay waved to a surprised Jesse. Gabby realized she was being rude. Not even that mattered right now. Tears filled her eyes. All her plans had gone up in smoke.

In the ride share, she swiped at her tears. Here she was, crying over a man. Again. Except this time, the pain cut her heart into a thousand pieces, leaving her nothing but misery.

***

Sawyer swore when he saw the time. He'd been tied up on the phone with the wine vendor, and it was almost eleven. He sighed and walked out of the office.

"Are they finally satisfied?" Eric asked. "The vendor was insistent they talk only to you."

"More or less. I'm glad I've set up another vendor." Sawyer glanced at table one. It was empty. "Damn," he muttered.

"She left," Eric commented.

"Yeah. She told me she couldn't stay too late as she has a flight home tomorrow." Sawyer had hoped to spend more time with her tonight and see how she felt about a long-distance relationship.

"Sorry about that."

"Not your fault." Sawyer pulled out his cell phone and sent a quick text.

Hey, Gabby, sorry I got tied up. Have a safe flight home tomorrow and let me know when you land. I already miss you. S.

He sent the message. Depending on what time they left, she might already be asleep. He had kept her up late last night. Had it only been last night? Sawyer felt like they'd known each other for years rather than just a weekend.

The sound of raised voices pulled him out of his thoughts. Glancing down at the floor, he saw two guys arguing. It was going to be one of those nights. Damn. He slipped his phone in his pocket and went to take care of the problem.

***

"I'm going to miss you," Lindsay said, hugging Gabby good-bye at the airport drop off.

"Me too." Gabby hugged her friend tight. Last night, Lindsay had sat with her while she cried over Sawyer. Lindsay was angry on her behalf.

"I've got to go."

"Call me when you get home." Lindsay gave her one last squeeze before letting her go.

"I will." Gabby grabbed her bag and walked through the double doors, keeping her sunglasses on to hide her tear-ravaged eyes. Her limbs felt heavy, as if something weighed them down. She looked at the self-service kiosk, decided she didn't have the brain power to deal with it, and walked to the check-in counter. Thankfully, there wasn't a line.

"Good morning," the cheery clerk said.

"Morning," Gabby mumbled, pulling her glasses off, putting her bag on the metal scale, and handing the clerk her license. Finding her boarding pass on her phone, she showed it to the clerk.

"Nice to have you flying with us today, Ms. Maxwell. Is San Francisco your final destination?"

"Yes."

"And just the one bag?"

"That's right."

The woman typed some things in the computer and frowned. Gabby's heart sank. The plane had showed on-time when they left Lindsay's place. The clerk typed a few more things. "Is there something wrong?"

"Oh no, ma'am. Give me just a minute." More typing and the computer spit out the luggage tag and a new boarding pass. "Here we go." She put the luggage tag on and sent the bag on its way. "You're at gate N14, security is to your left and once through follow the signs. You'll need to take the tram to the gate. Have a wonderful flight."

"Thank you." Gabby grabbed the boarding pass and her license. She glanced at the paper in her hand. "Ummm, excuse me."

"Is there something wrong?"

"Yes. This says I can go through pre-check."

"Yes, ma'am." The woman leaned closer. "I've upgraded you to first class."

Gabby blinked. "First class?"

"Yes. To be honest, you look like you could use a little pampering."

Gabby almost laughed. She'd cried most of the night, the cold compress could only do so much for her eyes. "Thank you."

"Anytime."

With her sunglasses covering her eyes again, Gabby walked away. Security was a breeze, and she made it to her gate easily. Finding a seat, she pulled out her phone, checking for activity. Just last night's text from Sawyer. A sigh escaped her lips. *Buck up.* Nothing was going to come of her mooning over Sawyer. He lied, and that's all there was to it. He knew money was a trigger for her, and he'd lied about it.

Somewhere in the dregs of last night's pity party, Gabby had realized she still wanted to move to Seattle. She was in a job she didn't like, and everything in her condo reminded her of her ex. It was time for a change, and she'd just have to make sure she steered well clear of the Vault and its...owner. Once she got home, she'd immerse herself in packing and give her notice. Job or no job. Lindsay was her closest friend, and she wanted to make her home where Lindsay was. It was time to do something new and different.

It would help her forget all about him. Her heart pounded, a painful reminder that she didn't want to forget him. She hated how he'd gotten past all her defenses and, in such a short time, become someone special to her. Beyond special. And he'd been lying to her the entire time.

Tears welled. *Enough.* She was done crying over him. Time to take back her power.

Chapter Six

♥

Sawyer paced around his office. Radio silence from Gabby and he didn't like it. He checked the flights to San Francisco. All had left on time. He hoped she'd text him to say she made it home okay.

"Ummm, Sawyer, there's a woman here to see you," one of the bouncers said.

Sawyer's mood perked up. "Great." He made his way downstairs. When he got to the bar area, he was surprised to see Lindsay sitting on a bar stool.

"Lindsay."

"About time."

The coldness in her voice almost made him take a step back. "Is everything okay? Is Gabby okay?" His heart stuttered at the thought of Gabby hurt.

"You're an ass, you know that? I want an explanation, and I want it now."

Sawyer was confused. "Explain what, Lindsay?"

"How you could hurt my best friend the way you did."

"Hurt Gabby?" He'd never hurt her. He was half in love with her. Shock ran through him. Half in love? Probably more than that. They'd been apart for less than twenty-four hours. He missed her more than he had any other person in his life. "I have no idea what you're talking about."

"You lied to her." Lindsay poked her finger at his chest.

A sliver of dread zipped up his spine. Sawyer tilted his head. "How did I lie to her?"

"Oh come on, Sawyer." Lindsay waved her hands in the air. "The Vault. You're the owner, not the manager you told Gabby you were."

"I'll admit that's true. How did you figure it out?" He wasn't going to lie. In a way, it was a relief that Lindsay and Gabby knew the truth.

"Jesse let it slip last night. It's not his fault, so don't blame him."

"I won't. Is that why Gabby won't answer my texts?"

Lindsay gave him a curt nod. "I'm glad she's not. You hurt her, and you don't deserve her."

He stood there for a moment. "You're right. I don't deserve her, but that doesn't matter. She's important to me."

"So important that you lied?"

"I didn't technically lie; I just kept some things to myself."

"Yeah. Like the fancy apartment Lindsay told me was a perk of your job. I bet that's yours as well."

Guilt flashed through his body. "It is."

"Damn it, Sawyer. Gabby doesn't care about your money. She cares about you, and you abused that. Plus, you lied about the one thing she just got done unraveling her life from. Money."

He opened his mouth to defend himself, but he couldn't. She was right. He should have told Gabby the truth on Sunday, but he didn't. He had chosen the selfish road, preferring anonymity rather than risk the usual butt kissing because he had money. Except his instincts told him Gabby wouldn't treat him like that. But he'd never given her a chance to prove herself. He'd thrown her in with every other woman without giving her a chance. He was a complete ass. "What do I do to get her to talk to me?"

Lindsay side-eyed him. "Why should I help you?"

"I love her."

Lindsay's eyes widened. "Grovel."

"How can I do that if she won't talk to me?" He was willing to do anything to get Gabby to talk to him.

Lindsay stared at him, and something must have told her how serious he was, because her features softened. "You've got a mountain to climb."

"Help me climb it because I'd do anything for Gabby."

"All right," Lindsay said. "We need someplace quiet to talk."

"Let's go to my office." Sawyer stood and guided Lindsay upstairs.

"First things first," Lindsay said, poking him in the chest. Hard. "You hurt my best friend again and I'll roast your nuts."

Sawyer held up both hands in surrender. "I'm sure there will be others who will help you." He had no intention of hurting Gabby again, even though he hadn't meant to the first time. No. He wanted her in his life.

***

Gabby closed the front door to her apartment and leaned against it. She was tired. Her flight had been at nine, it was now almost one. She'd put her phone in airplane mode, but when she landed and reconnected on the network, her phone nearly blew up.

Texts from Sawyer. She wasn't ready to talk with him yet. After sending a quick text to Lindsay to let her know she'd landed, she ordered a ride share to take her home. Her apartment felt dreary, like all the joy had been sucked out of it. She'd never been completely happy here, but she'd been content. Now, it just reminded her of every failure in her life.

Wheeling her suitcase into the bedroom, she left it by the door and went into the bathroom. A quick shower would make her feel better. On the flight home, she'd thought a lot about what she and Lindsay had discussed.

She was tired of working long hours, and she wanted something different. Opening her own place would mean long hours again, but it would be her place, not working for someone else. Until she could afford that, some of the jobs she applied for would give her more freedom.

Gabby slipped on her favorite yoga pants and a t-shirt and made her way to her small living room. Once there, she opened her laptop. No time like the present. She quickly typed up a letter of resignation and sent it to her boss at the restaurant.

Tomorrow she'd take a signed copy to him as well. No one was going to be happy about it, but it was time. Two weeks was plenty of time for her to pack up her place and arrange to move in with Lindsay.

Her stomach grumbled. She hadn't eaten much today, only a bagel at the airport. Pushing to her feet, she went in her tiny kitchen and opened the fridge. Well, darn. There wasn't much there. She hadn't gone shopping before she left.

She put on the tea kettle while she tried to decide what she wanted to have delivered. Once her tea was brewing, she sat down in the overstuffed chair she loved, her feet curled underneath her. Gabby began typing on her tablet, making a list of things she needed to do. Half an hour later, she glanced at the list and sipped her now almost cold tea.

Not a bad list. The thing was, could she do it? She pulled up her bank account and noted the balance in her checking and saving accounts. She'd given her two weeks' notice, so she'd have one more paycheck from her job.

She wouldn't have rent if she lived with Lindsay. Gabby shook her head. There would still be rent but not as much as she was paying here. She calculated in food and other things. Okay, she could go without a job for about two months.

Could she set up her own business in two months? Doubtful, but that didn't mean she couldn't work. One of the jobs she'd been looking at was a personal chef. Mainly for dinner and dinner parties. While she checked out the job, she couldn't resist and put Sawyer's name into the search.

There was article after article, so she started reading about his days in tech and how he'd sold his company and then bought The Vault. There was very little gossip about him, mainly business information.

A yawn escaped. She'd been up early this morning so Lindsay could get her to the airport. Maybe a little nap would help. Scooching down in the chair, she set her tablet aside and closed her eyes. She'd rest here for a few minutes.

***

An insistent knocking brought Gabby awake. "Just a second," she yelled. A groan left her lips as she tried to straighten her body. She'd fallen asleep in the chair, and now everything hurt. She shifted, put her legs straight out, and wiggled her feet.

At least that wasn't too bad. She braced with her hands and pushed up out of the chair. Her legs were steady. Another good thing. She made her way to her front door and looked out the peep hole.

"Sawyer?" Her voice squeaked.

"Please open the door, Gabby."

Her fingers curled around the knob, her other hand on the security locks. She froze. Did she want to talk to Sawyer? Yes. No! Oh, heck. He'd come down here. She might as well hear him out. Though there was nothing he could say that would change the hurt she felt.

Was she going to do this? Yes. She turned the knob and pulled the door open, blocking entry with her body. "I don't know what you want."

His hair was disheveled, his shirt wrinkled, along with his pants. It had only been a little over a day, but he looked as if he hadn't slept in days. This wasn't the sophisticated, elegant man she was used to seeing.

"Can we talk? Please?"

Another please. Even his voice was scratchy. Fine. She'd hear him out, before sending him on his way.

"Come in." She let go of the door and stepped back. Her heart was hurt, but Sawyer looked like he was hurting too. And she didn't take joy in that.

Sawyer entered, and her apartment shrank. It wasn't that big to begin with, but now it was extra small. She could smell his cologne. An image of him and her in bed together flashed in her mind. "Maybe this isn't a good idea."

He glanced around her apartment. "Maybe not. It looks like I woke you up. I saw a café around the corner; why don't we go there and have a chat?"

"I'm not sure what we have to talk about." She really wasn't. He'd lied to her.

"Please, Gabby. Let me explain, and if you want nothing to do with me after that, I'll walk away."

She blinked. He was giving her an out. This wasn't the take-charge man she was used to. "All right. Let me change clothes, and I'll meet you there in twenty."

His face lit up, and he lifted his hand. His fingers brushed her cheek, and it was all Gabby could do not to press her cheek against his hand. "See you soon." He turned and left her apartment.

She stood there for a moment before turning and going to the bedroom closet. Something to wear. Jeans and a shirt. Grabbing them, she went into her bathroom. How had Sawyer known where to find her?

Lindsay was more than likely the one who told him where she lived, and she must have had a good reason. Maybe she should call Lindsay to find out what Sawyer said to her. Gabby shook her head. No, this was her decision to make, no one else's. She quickly cleaned up and dressed.

She grabbed her purse and made sure her keys and cell were in it before she left her apartment. Her hands shook as she locked the door. Was she nervous? Oh yes. She was curious what Sawyer had to say, but she was also apprehensive. What excuse was there for what he'd done?

Was she crazy to give him another chance? Maybe, but seeing him at her door had been a shock. He wasn't the Sawyer she remembered from twenty-four hours ago. Oh, her body still went on alert and wanted to sink into his embrace. But her brain noticed the lines of strain around his eyes and the stiffness of his movements.

The little bell on the door to the café jingled as she opened it. She waved to the ladies behind the counter before she looked for Sawyer. She loved this quaint café. There he was, sitting at a table in the back. Gabby made her way over.

He stood when he saw her. Ever the gentleman. "Thank you for coming," he said as she sat down.

"I'm not sure I should have." Gabby folded her hands into her lap.

"Hey, Gabby. Coffee or something else?" the waitress asked.

"Coffee, please." Her cup was poured, and Sawyer's was topped off.

"Would you like to order now?"

Gabby ate here often enough to know the menu, but she wasn't feeling hungry just yet. "Just coffee for now."

"Same for me."

"Okay, wave me down when you're ready." She smiled at Sawyer and walked away.

Sawyer stared at her. "Now that you're here, I don't know what to say."

Gabby had plenty to say but, instead, asked the question that was burning a hole in her brain. "Why did you lie to me?"

He winced. "I didn't technically lie. I do manage the club, but I didn't mention I owned it. I didn't see any reason to. We'd just met, and I had to be sure." Sawyer placed his palms on the table.

"Sure of what?" Curiosity got the better of her. She wanted to know his reasoning.

"After I sold my tech startup, I dated a woman. She knew who I was, and it started off well. She made me believe she wasn't after my money. It started slowly, she began asking me for more and more items. I finally caved and gave her one of my credit cards, and she went on a spending spree. When I canceled the card, she became angry. She flat out told me all she cared about was my money and what I could buy for her. Since then, I've been very cautious."

Gabby glanced out the window. "That's horrible. I can understand why you'd be cautious."

His hand closed over hers, but she pulled away, not quite ready to forgive him. Even if all she wanted right now was his hands on her. His lips on her. His heart beating the same as hers.

"You're not like that. I realized it within minutes of meeting you."

"How?" She was curious.

"The first sign was that you didn't recognize me when I introduced myself."

"Why should I?"

Sawyer chuckled. "See. Your friend Lindsay figured that out faster than you did. When I learned you didn't live in Seattle, I began to understand why you didn't know my name."

"I was shocked when Jesse said you owned The Vault. I have to admit I did a quick internet search on you when I got home. But nearly all of the information was business, almost nothing personal. Why would that make you so recognizable? I don't understand."

"You read about VoltAir Technologies?"

"Yes." Her eyes widened as if she realized what it meant. "I only skimmed the articles, and the ones I read didn't mention money."

"I sold it off five years ago, and it made me an instant billionaire. And that's when all the parasites started coming out of the woodwork."

"What happened?" She reached out and squeezed his hand.

"Everyone wanted a piece of me, including Gina."

"The woman you mentioned?"

"Yes. I hated being defined by my money. So I basically went underground. Eric and I bought The Vault. It was still a little crazy after we opened—with people trying to curry favor—but they learned quickly I wasn't going to bite."

"And Gina?" Her heart hurt for him. Her ex had treated her like a bank but nothing like what Sawyer must have gone through.

"When I refused to give in to her demands, she tried a few other things, but when I wouldn't bite, she finally left. Not that it bothered me. By that time, I was tired of her. When I met you…"

"You were worried I'd go crazy over your money."

His eyes lit. "Yes, but you were the opposite. I saw it from the start. Gabby, you were so down to earth. When I said I was a manager, you didn't look down on me, but instead, we started talking about how hard a job it is."

"And Saturday?"

"I knew I needed to tell you. Selfishly, I held back. I wanted to spend time with you and show you Seattle. Knowing you're a chef, I decided to pull out all the stops with the food tour, shops that would appeal to you, the underground tour, and dinner at the Space Needle."

"All things to seduce me." Her voice was soft.

He shook his head. "All things you would be likely to enjoy with me. You don't know how hard it was for me not to buy you everything you looked at. I wanted to. I wanted to see you smile and be carefree. And at the end of dinner, if you had wanted to go back to Lindsay's place, I would've taken you there. Even if it meant a very cold shower when I got home."

She believed him. Sawyer wasn't one to hold a woman against her will. "The car and driver?"

"He's an employee of a local company; I do use them a lot."

"The apartment belongs to you?"

"Yes. I didn't want to frighten you away."

Gabby shifted in her seat. "When I told you about my ex, why didn't you say something?"

"I didn't know how. Guilt ate at me, but I didn't know how to come clean without breaking your trust." He looked down at their hands, still entwined. "In the end, I broke it anyway."

"You did."

His hand tightened around hers. "Tell me what I need to do to make this up to you, and I'll do it. Just name it."

"Give away all your money," she blurted out.

"Fine. I can do that."

"No," Gabby yelled, causing people to look at them. "I didn't mean that. Sawyer, you earned that money. Nothing will convince me otherwise that you didn't give your electronics company your all. The money you earned from selling it was justified."

"I will give it all up for you."

"I don't want you to. I want you to be happy."

"I'll only be happy if you're in my life."

She closed her eyes. "That's not true."

"But it is." Sawyer released her hand, moved around the table and knelt next to her. "Gabby, I'm nothing without you. I'm usually not impulsive, yet with you, I am."

Tears filled her eyes. He'd come here to make things right. She'd been home, what? A few hours and here he was, humbling himself for her. No one had ever done that before.

"Get up, Sawyer."

"I'm not done groveling yet."

Gabby laughed and waved her hand at his empty seat. "Sit down, and we'll finish this talk, but quit making a spectacle of the two of us."

He glanced around, and the entire restaurant watched them. Sawyer grinned. "They're watching me win back the heart of the woman I love."

"What?" Her mouth dropped open. "You can't love me."

"Why not?"

"Because..." She had to think. "We just met."

"I knew Saturday you were the woman for me."

She shook her head. "I don't believe in love at first sight."

"I don't either, but you broke the mold."

Gabby didn't know what to say. She really didn't believe love could happen that fast, even if her heart argued with her on the point.

"I know this is all too soon, and I get it. All I'm asking is you give us a chance."

She swallowed. "I can do that."

Relief flashed over his features.

"But don't lie to me again."

"I won't. I promise."

"All right. Let's get some food and we can talk some more."

***

Sawyer took a deep breath. It felt like the first good breath he'd taken in hours. Gabby forgave him. He was humbled and honored. Now to win back her trust. He'd have to tread carefully for a while. Not that he planned to violate her trust again.

"Why did you sell your company?" she asked after their food arrived.

"I was bored." He grinned. "I'd done all I wanted to do."

"Why a club?"

"That was a happy accident. My friend Eric had been looking around for a new business venture and came to me. We toured the building and loved the idea of turning it into a club."

"What was it before?"

"A restaurant, so we had a kitchen, and the rest was easy enough to change out."

"The restaurant had a second floor?"

"Yeah, they used it for storage, so we opened it up. Put the DJ upstairs along with our office, and an area for people we invite who don't want to be on the main floor."

"It looks great. I'm glad you enjoy having the club."

Sawyer shifted. "I was restless until I met you. It's like everything fell into place."

"You give me too much credit."

He shook his head. "How do I explain what a breath of fresh air you are? I was struck by your laughter when I first saw you. So carefree. And the dancing. We fit together like we'd known each other for ages. And as we talked, it was as if I'd known you forever. You didn't care what I did for a living. You didn't think you were better than others."

"That isn't how I'm wired."

"Right. Saturday, you were worried about how much money I spent, but the joy and excitement on your face was worth a thousand times that. Do you know how hard it was for me not to buy you things?"

"Is that why you were antsy in some of the stores? I thought you might be bored."

"Oh no. I wanted to go behind you and buy everything you put back on the shelves. I wanted you to have every spice, sauce, knife, and anything else you wanted. I wanted to spoil you."

"You did. No one has ever done something like what you did for me. You saw me and designed a day around what I loved. The shops, dinner, and being with you. You were the one who mattered, not what you could buy me."

"I know. That's part of what makes you so special."

Gabby looked down at her empty plate. "I'm not sure I should mention this to you now, but—"

"What?" His heart skipped a beat.

"I think I told you I haven't been happy in my job."

"Yes, you mentioned it."

"Well, Lindsay and I talked, and I'm moving to Seattle to do something different."

"But you love being a chef." She couldn't give up a part of herself. He wouldn't let her.

"I do. And I want to continue, only in a different capacity."

"How?" He was curious about her plans. He would support her no matter what. Just having her closer to him would make him happy, and he would make sure that happiness was reciprocated.

"I've been looking at private chef jobs."

He hadn't even thought of that. He knew some of his business associates had their own chefs. For him personally, he either ordered out or if needed, had someone cater. "How would that work for you?"

"Honestly, I'm not sure. I've never done anything like that, but from the job postings I've seen, I'm more than qualified. I've even applied for a couple of them already."

"That's great. So, if you get one, you'll move?"

"No."

Sawyer frowned.

"I'm moving regardless if I get the job or not. I miss my best friend, and the Seattle area has so much to offer. And to make it better, you are there."

"I don't want you to move because of me. I'm willing to do the long-distance thing. I can fly down here anytime."

"But now you won't have to spend the money. I'll live with Lindsay, and it won't be as expensive as living alone. I don't have much here, so moving isn't an issue."

"Are you sure this is what you want?"

"Yes." She smiled. "I need a change. Plus, I'm already half in love with you, so it all makes perfect sense."

He wasn't going to argue with her.

Gabby's cell rang, and she grabbed it out of her purse. "Excuse me for a second." She put the phone up to her ear. "Hello." There was a pause. He could hear a male voice, but not the words. "Oh yes. Really? Ummm... Yes, I can do a virtual interview. Can you give me thirty minutes? I'm just finishing up on a late lunch out. Great. Thank you." She set her phone down and stared at him.

"Job interview?" He had no doubt that's what the call was about.

"Yes. So unexpected, but they read my application and wanted to grab me before anyone else did."

"Let's get back to your place so you can get ready for the interview." Sawyer waved to their waitress and paid the bill.

An hour later, Gabby started at him. "I can't believe it."

"I can." He'd stayed in the kitchen area of her apartment while she took the interview. With her place being so small, he'd overheard the entire thing. It had been a great success.

"I've got the contract. Pull a chair over and read it with me, please. I'd appreciate your opinion."

Sawyer grabbed the other chair and sat next to her. He was so happy for her. She'd given her credentials but didn't overplay her strengths or try to make herself out to be something she wasn't. That was his Gabby.

Together, they read the contract. When they got to the pay portion, Gabby stopped. "They can't be serious."

"They can." The amount didn't surprise him. Excellent private or personal chefs were hard to come by. "Actually, that is very reasonable. Three to four hours a day, weekends off. Extra pay for dinner parties or weekends."

"But..." Gabby pulled up a calculator on her phone and put in some numbers. "That's as much as I'm being paid now for less work."

"Yes, it is."

"I..." She shook her head. "I've got so much I need to do."

"You are going to accept the job?"

"I am." She leaned over and kissed him. "Here's to a new beginning."

"I'm all for that. Tell me what you need me to do?"

"I've already given notice at my job. I need figure out what I'm keeping and what is going, plus pack and..."

Tears filled her eyes. "If I hadn't met you, none of this would be happening."

"Wrong. You would have done just fine. You're the one who got the ball rolling. I'm here to support you."

"But what about the club?"

"Eric can handle it for a few weeks. I'll owe him big time, but I can deal with that."

"This has all happened so fast."

"It's meant to be."

"I'm beginning to think it is." She glanced around. "This place is small. But if you don't mind sharing a double bed. You can stay here."

"I would love to share your bed, and your apartment is fine. It's homey, and I like it. This will also give me a chance to check out clubs in the area and see what they're doing. I need to stay on top of the trends."

Gabby laughed. "My one weekend in Seattle is the best thing that has happened to me."

"Me too. And I will be with you each step of the way on your new journey. When you're ready, we can take the next steps in our relationship."

"I already love you more now than I did an hour ago."

"That's good because I'm not letting you go. You're mine."

***

Thank you for reading *One Weekend in Seattle*. I will have two new books out in May and June. It's a duology set on an adult ranch. Coming later in the year is my new series: Fantasies, Inc. They will make your fantasies come true—even if you didn't know you had them. Alpha men and independent women who explore together and find love. Keep an eye out for information about these books in my newsletter. You can sign up by going to my website: https://www.marietuhart.com/join-mailing-list.htmlIf you enjoyed *One Weekend in Seattle,* check out Temporary Nanny for the Tycoon:Blake Ellington doesn't need the complication of taking care of his niece in the middle of delicate business negations, but what choice does he have. His mother is in the hospital, and his sister out of the country. He has no idea of how to handle a baby, let alone one that won't stop crying. With an outrageous amount offered for the nanny job, Abby will have enough to support herself as she goes after her dream of being a full-time pastry chef. She can't refuse. She didn't expect to find her client so irresistible, but he is a client, and she has a rule about not getting involved. Besides, she doesn't need a man in her life. Her job is to take care of the baby, and that's what she plans to do. Until Blake kisses her.

About the author

Marie Tuhart lives in the beautiful Pacific Northwest with her two dogs, Tommy and Trina. Marie brings to life contemporary approachable alpha heroes and the spunky women who take them to task. Her high-heat, emotional books, many with BDSM elements, inviting the reader to slid the silky scarves between their fingers, fell the kiss of a flogger on their flesh in breathless anticipation of what or who will come next. Embrace the temptation and enjoy a happily ever after that's always about the heroine.

Check out Marie's website at: https://www.marietuhart.com

Other Books by Marie Tuhart

Tempt (Wicked Sanctuary Series)

Entice (Wicked Sanctuary Series)

Seduce (Wicked Sanctuary Series)

Ravish (Wicked Sanctuary Series)

Possess (Wicked Sanctuary Series)

Tantalize (Wicked Sanctuary Series)

Edged (Wicked Sanctuary Series)

Unmasked (Wicked Sanctuary Series)

Too Hot (Wicked Sanctuary Series)

Wicked Sanctuary Novellas:

Untamed

Power Play

Claiming Rose

Standalone Books:

Embracing Desire